A TOUCH OF MALICE

KARI LEE TOWNSEND

OLIVER-HEBER BOOKS

To my family, both immediate and extended, I am so blessed to have you in my life. Family means everything to me, and I'm very lucky to have most of mine still around. I don't take that for granted. Love you all!

CHAPTER 1

"So, Ballas, when are you going to put me out of my misery and make this official?" Nikos Stevens stood tall and gorgeous in his sport coat and jeans.

He was so dreamy, with thick, wavy coffee-colored hair blowing in the autumn breeze, his olive skin glowing, and his piercing blue eyes holding me captive. He sipped his coffee while leaning against the other side of the fence separating our backyards. This had become both our morning routines. His huge St. Bernard, Wolfgang, stomped around the lawn to do his business before Nik left for work at the police station.

I slowly walked down from my deck to join him on my side of the fence, my sensible pumps crunching the fallen leaves as I made my way over. My finicky calico cat, Miss Priss, lounged on the deck railing up above, turning her nose up at Wolfgang as he whined to be near her.

I wore my standard suit and long blond hair in my usual chignon, making me feel organized and in control. I came to a stop and sipped my organic green tea, pondering how to reply. I didn't have much time before I had to head into work at Full Disclosure myself. I had my new fall collection of Kalli Originals lingerie to launch and was excited to get started.

"Last I checked, Detective, we already went on a date." I smoothed the front of my jacket three times before reaching over the fence to hold his large masculine hand, mine looking so pale and small wrapped inside of his.

"Last I checked, Darlin', one date does not make us an official couple. Besides, that was quite a while ago. If I didn't know better, I would think you were avoiding me." He winked, his full lips tipping up a hair and looking sexy as all get out surrounded by heavy whiskers on his square jawline. He lowered his head, never breaking eye contact, and kissed my hand, lingering longer than necessary. *Oh, the things I would officially do if you were mine. You have no idea, my love.*

"You know I wouldn't avoid you. We've both been busy." I squeezed his hand once and then gently pulled mine away, feeling the blush creep across my cheeks.

I didn't even try to be discreet anymore. I set my teacup on the fencepost and rubbed my hands together with the hand sanitizer that was always on my person while taking three deep breaths. *He* had no idea I could hear his every thought whenever we touched, ever since I fell out of my best friend Jaz's loft at her clothing boutique and hit my head. I didn't know if I could physically survive 'official' togetherness all the time.

The ability to read minds was both a blessing and a curse.

"You okay?" Detective Dreamy puckered his forehead in concern. "You look flushed. Do you have a fever?"

I searched my mind for excuses. It was fall and already chilly in Clearview Connecticut, so I definitely wasn't overheated. I was too young for a hot flash, so there went that explanation. I wasn't prepared to tell him about my mind reading ability because he was the first man who hadn't been scared off by my quirks.

An OCD germaphobe wasn't exactly everyone's cup of tea.

I didn't want to jinx that by having him think I was totally crazy, even though hearing his thoughts was the only way I stayed out of my own head long enough for him to kiss me. The very thing that made me a freak of nature, made our relationship possible.

I threw up my hands at a loss. "I'm nervous, okay?" I finally said. "We're perfect just the way we are. Why do we have to risk messing with what is happening between us by putting a name to what we are? I just don't want anything to ruin what we're building. Besides, we've only just started to date. Why rush things?"

"That's true, but you can't say we haven't been through a lot together. The kind of life and death experiences that speed things up and make a person think about their future. What's important to them." His gaze softened. "For me, that's you. But I won't push."

"At least we'll have more privacy now that Jaz has finally moved in with Boomer," I said as a consolation of sorts.

Jazlyn Alvarez was my best friend. Supermodel tall, gorgeous like her mother, and smart like her banker father. She had broken most of the men's hearts in town at one time or another until finally falling for Boomer Matheson. The house was hers.

She'd let me live with her while Nik rented out the other half. He was right. A lot had happened with two murders, friends and family becoming suspects, and me nearly dying twice. I knew I wanted him in my life, but I didn't like change.

The future was scary.

"Privacy is good. We can be private together." He wagged his eyebrows.

"Look, this is the first time I've ever lived on my own," I tried to explain further as I looked at him, letting all my feelings show. "I'm enjoying it."

"I understand what you're saying, but don't get too comfortable. Who knows how long Jaz will last living in a bachelor pad with a guy like Detective Matheson?"

I looked at my watch and then picked up my now cold tea. "Oh, trust me, she's already put her stamp on his place."

Nik snorted. "I heard."

I frowned. "What does that mean?"

His smile vanished and eyes widened for a moment. "Nothing. Nothing at all. Forget I said anything."

"Well, it's a little late for that." I stood a little straighter, not about to let my best friend get hurt.

"I'm just saying Jaz is a strong, independent, force to be reckoned with on her own. Add in Chanel and Versace, and Boomer's world is completely different. It's an adjustment, that's all." Chanel and Versace were the full-size poodles they had adopted after their former owners were arrested.

I hated to admit it, but he had a point. "That's another reason why I don't want to move too fast," I pointed out. "We're totally different people with vastly different habits and ideas of cleanliness. Not to mention our pets are not exactly the best of friends." Prissy hissed right on cue, baring her fangs, and Wolfgang tipped back his head and let out a pathetic howl, drool dripping down his massive face.

I gagged.

I had an automatic, self-cleaning litterbox that cost a fortune. I had all I could do to empty that. At least there was no scooping. I shuddered at the size of Wolfgang's pooper scooper. Not a chance was I going near that thing.

"Okay, okay, I get it." Nik scrubbed a hand through his hair, clearly frustrated, but still apparently determined to make us work as an actual couple. "Our situation is complicated. You've got a point."

"Or two, or three, or four."

"Please, Ballas, don't overthink this one." His eyes gentled as he looked at me with an emotion I couldn't quite identify. "We've got a good thing going."

I paused for a long moment and then replied, "Agreed, Detective. I don't know exactly what I want for my future, but I do know I want you in it." I leaned over and kissed him briefly on the lips. "Everything in my life is finally going well. I don't plan to let anything get in the way of that."

"Good. I can live with that." He nodded once, glanced at his watch, and then whistled for Wolfgang to go inside. He looked at me once more. "Kalli Ballas, would you care to join me for dinner this evening?"

I fluttered my hand to my chest and batted my eyelashes. "Another date? Why, Detective Stevens, I thought you'd never ask." I laughed and smiled from ear-to-ear before saying, "I would love to." I added a wink, and he raised a brow as a beaming smile spread across his hopeful, handsome face.

I walked away, feeling happy. Feeling good. I frowned. Feeling *too* good.

Every time I had ever felt this good in the past, something always happened to make me realize my happiness was too good to be true. My anxiety started to build, so I squared my shoulders and inhaled a deep breath three times, then raised my chin a notch. I decided *not* to overthink this one, just like I'd promised Detective Dreamy.

For both our sakes.

~

APHRODITE'S WAS MY PARENTS' other baby. The goddess of love, beauty, and all things Greek filled every inch of space, with plenty of marble statues scattered about just short of overkill. Everyone loved Aphrodite's with her beautiful Greek culture on display and food prepared with skill and pride.

Nik and I sat at a table, having dinner after a perfect day. There wasn't any crime going on in Clearview at the moment. My fall line launch went off without a hitch. And I was on another date with Detective Dreamy. Life didn't get any better than this. I was being silly earlier, worrying that everything positive in my life could be too good to be true. I deserved to be happy just like everyone else, and I was determined to stop thinking so negatively.

What could possibly go wrong?

My cousin, Eleni, worked at my parents' restaurant as a waitress, and her sister Frona was the dishwasher. When they could keep her in the back, that is. Frona had fallen off an apple cart years ago, hitting her head, and hadn't been the same since. Eleni adjusted her long black ponytail then scrubbed her hands three times before picking out a couple of pastries with a clean napkin, placing them on a sanitized plate, and then setting it on our table for us to share.

She knew me well.

"These are on me for two of my favorite people who would make a really cute couple, by the way."

And there you go. Strike one for this evening.

There was no escaping friends and my massive family, who owned half the businesses in this town. Now that Nik and I were dating, the whole town was on a mission. I gave her a pointed look.

"Just sayin'." She blew me a kiss and winked at Nik, then snagged a skipping Frona's arm as she passed by without missing a beat, her lopsided pony-tails bouncing as Eleni guided her to the back.

"That was sweet of your cousin." Nik grinned and sank his teeth into a flaky Filo pastry, giving me an innocent look.

"Mmmhmmm," was all I said, eying him suspiciously. I wouldn't be surprised if he'd put her up to that. So much for not pressuring me.

"There's my baby." Ma came out of the kitchen after fussing over our meal personally, making a bee-line toward our table with bright eyes full of pride and arms flailing about. Her big poof of teased black hair was secured in her usual beehive, with an apron tied over her polyester pants and blouse.

I loved my big Greek family, but sometimes they were a bit much. I was Ma's and Pop's only child after they got lucky through adoption, but I couldn't be more different from them. Pale where they were dark, introverted while they were anything but, and I didn't like to be touched while they were bear hugs and smooches all day long.

"Thanks, Ma, dinner was delicious," I said and meant it. She was a fabulous cook. I knew my way around the kitchen, I simply chose to use organic whole foods and eat clean.

"You no worry. You start cooking like me instead of the bird food you make. That'll keep your man happy." She winked at Nik. "A big hearty man like yours can't live off nuts and seeds alone."

I sighed. Strike two for the evening.

"He's not my anything yet, Ma." I discreetly glanced around at all the eyes on us and lowered my voice. "We're only on our second date."

"Title Schmitle." She waved her hands in front of my face like jazz hands. "He's a man, and he's here with you." She patted my shoulder then let her hand rest there. "That makes him your man." *And a handsome man he is. She takes after me. It's in the genes. Maybe it's time I talked to her about the birds and the—*

"Okay, then, I think we're done here." I dropped my napkin then bent over to pick it up, and Ma's hand fell away, thank the gods. Genes Schmenes, I was adopted. I didn't take after anyone, that I knew anyway. "You ready to go, Detective? I think I've had enough for one night."

Ma's face puckered up like a pickle.

I tried not to roll my eyes and smiled a little too bright. "Enough food for the night." I rubbed my stomach. "I'm stuffed."

She beamed. "That's my girl. You need to eat more." She pointed her finger at my face. "You too skinny. Men no like skinny. They like curves. Trust me." She moved her hips like a belly dancer.

I nearly fell off my chair.

Nik's eyes twinkled with amusement, and his lips twitched with the effort not to grin. He knew better. "Sure thing, Babe," he practically purred at me in response to my question.

Ma let out a half giggle, half screech.

I narrowed my eyes.

He refused to look at me as he directed his comment at my ma this time. "The food was delicious as always, Mrs. Ballas. Your Moussaka was better than Ma's, but don't tell her I said that."

Nikos Stevens was only half-Greek because his father was British, but the Greek side of his ma's Pagonis family was as big as mine. Nik inherited his mother's swarthy dark looks and his father's large size and crystal blue eyes. When he was Detective Stevens, he was all business. When he was Nik, he was sweet and made me want to make things official. When he was Nikos the Greek, I wanted to wipe the smug smile off his chiseled face.

Ma beamed and stood a little straighter, fanning her pink cheeks. "Oh, go on with you now. You too much, but you no worry. It will be our little secret. Now, get my daughter home safe at a respectable hour. She's precious cargo, you know."

"Ma, I'm not a teenager. I'm twenty-nine years old."

Her face sobered. "You're still my little girl."

The front door chimed as it opened, and in walked Nik's mother, Chloe, all chic and sophistication but still a Greek mama on a mission.

"Opa!" Ma thrust her hand in the air. "I have to go. Chloe and I have plans." Ma hustled away at a brisk pace, took off her apron, then the two of them sat at a table with heads bent, discussing *Zeus knew what* as they kept stealing glances at Nik and me.

"Great," Nik muttered and quickly paid the check.

"Look who's not so amused now." I sat back and crossed my arms, finally enjoying myself. "It's all fun and games until *your* mama shows up."

"Touché," he said, adding, "let's get out of here before things get any worse."

We stood and started making our way to the exit when the door opened again and in walked a woman who looked so familiar even from far away. She had golden blond hair and sea-green eyes with deep red lipstick, a tight red dress that clung to her curves, and a pair of matching red high heels. I felt like I'd seen her before, but I didn't know where.

I didn't ever remember seeing her in Clearview.

She looked around the room until her gaze landed on me. Her eyes widened as if she recognized me as well. As she walked over to me, I could see her better. She held out a hand, and I just stood there, gaping at her in return, my hand remaining firmly at my side.

She dropped her hand almost knowingly as she said, "Hi, Kalli Ballas. My name is Ruby Winehouse, and I'm your mother."

Chloe gasped, Ma fainted, and everyone started talking at once.

And there was strike three.

CHAPTER 2

Full Disclosure, Jaz's clothing boutique, was my second home. I practically lived in the loft upstairs where I created my designs. Located in the business district, the shop was a high-end clothing store that people from all over frequented. There was a burgundy microfiber sofa in the sitting area next to the dressing rooms, with decorative pin-striped pillows and a matching loveseat for shoppers to sit. Soft music played through the sound system, and the boutique smelled of lavender.

Debbie, the fashion designer intern Jaz had hired, was restocking the display of my new fall line while Jaz sat on a throw pillow on a stool behind the register, getting the drawer ready to cash people out. It was nice for both Jaz and me to have the extra help as our businesses were both booming these days.

I cringed at the pillow Jaz sat on.

She had a full cleaning crew, but I still secretly sanitized the furniture every chance I got. At least my loft studio was spotless, just the way I liked it, with a hand sanitizer stand at the top of the stairs just in case. No one was allowed up there. That was my only request when it came to my sanctuary, and Jaz had been gracious enough to give me that.

After last night's fiasco with my biological mother —no need for a DNA test; I look *exactly* like her— showing up out of the blue at my parents' restaurant, we ended up at Doc LaLone's office with Ma having heart palpitations.

I was still in shock.

I admittedly had sometimes wondered about my biological parents. What they might look like. Where they might live. What kind of jobs they had. Why they gave me up. For the most part, I didn't think of them at all. I honestly wouldn't trade my Big Fat Greek Family for anything, but they'd been forced to tell me after it became obvious.

I wasn't like the rest of them in looks or personality. Ma had never wanted to tell me I was adopted at all. She didn't like to think I wasn't one hundred percent hers, even though it didn't matter to me. I could never love her any less.

"I thought your adoption was closed?" Jaz's words jarred me from my thoughts as I came down from the loft and joined her by the register. It was almost time to open the boutique.

"It was." I shrugged.

"Then how on earth did...what's her name?"

I wrinkled my nose. "Ruby Winehouse."

Jaz raised her perfect eyebrows. "How did *Ruby* find you?"

"I guess she lives just one town over in Cloudsville. After the recent murders that happened around here, she saw me on the news. There's no mistaking she gave birth to me, but I am most definitely *not* her daughter. I'm nothing like her."

"I gathered as much. She's, um, very touchy feely

from what I've heard. Boomer said she already started making the rounds around town last night after she left Aphrodite's."

"That doesn't surprise me. Nik looked her up. She's a stripper for crying out loud. I don't even like to strip when I'm alone."

Jaz let out a half snort half giggle.

I scowled.

"Sorry." She slapped a palm over her grinning mouth.

I rolled my eyes. "I obviously take after my father, whoever he is."

Jaz puckered her forehead. "Did you ask her?"

"No. I was a little busy taking Ma to Doc's place after she fainted."

"How is she, anyway?"

"As feisty as ever." I refolded a few articles of clothing. "She woke up after fainting and started rapid firing questions and insults alternately at Ruby."

"Ah, so that's how you found out all that info."

"And *that's* what caused Ma's heart palpitations."

"I just don't get it. What could Ruby possibly want with you twenty-nine years after giving you up? From what Boomer told me, she doesn't exactly seem like the motherly type. Great genes, though. Lucky you. Boomer showed me a picture of her on his phone. That woman does *not* look fifty."

According to Nik, Ruby gave me up when she was twenty-one. Ma was a good decade older than her, looking every inch her age—her words not mine. Yet another reason she felt threatened by her, which was silly. My ma might be over the top and loud, but she was all mine and absolutely perfect to me.

The only mother I had ever known or wanted to know.

I didn't need a fake wannabe Mommy Dearest at my age. This Ruby Winehouse person meant nothing to me. I was grateful that her egg had helped give me life, but that was all she was to me. An egg donor.

"I don't know what she's up to, but I highly doubt she came to Clearview to start a relationship with me. The vibes I got from the moment she locked eyes with me made my skin crawl, and her voice had alarm bells ringing in my mind." My gut twisted into knots, and a feeling of pending doom filled me. "All I know for certain is that whatever Ruby Winehouse came here for can't be good."

~

THE PAST WEEK had been awful. Mommy Dearest had made the rounds all over town, making several enemies along the way. She'd dropped the act of wanting to get to know her long lost daughter pretty quickly. Apparently, she'd seen me on the news talking about the success of my clothing line.

Plain and simple, she was here for a handout.

The stress was getting to Ma, so I suggested we visit Aunt Tasoula's hair salon, Hera's Halo. Aunt Tasoula was my ma's sister, but they didn't look anything alike. She owned a hair salon, was half Ma's size, and tried to look much younger with black hair that was way too long and clothes that were far too tight.

Aunt Tasoula claimed Ma stole the goddess of love and beauty, Aphrodite, for her restaurant name. Aunt Tasoula chose the queen of the gods, Hera, for her hair salon, Hera's Halo. Their competitive spirits had them trying to outdo each other every chance they got, but they loved each other.

Right now, Ma needed her sister's support.

Ma picked up a magazine of celebrity gossip news to thumb through, then sat in a chair next to Winnie Wallaby, our new mail carrier. Winnie was Amazon tall and curvy, with long wavy auburn hair, friendly amber eyes, and an Australian accent. Ma didn't understand half the words Winnie said, but Ma had been on a mission to fix her up with my cousin Kosmos, who was Winnie's complete opposite: dark, short, and built like a tank.

The salon chairs looked like gold thrones, the capes like a queen's robe, and even the dryers were painted like crowns with precious gems adorning them.

"I have package of secret sauce for Kosmos' barbecue sandwich special. You carry for me. I make it worth your while." Ma Winked at Winnie.

"That sounds like a ripper!" Winnie spoke in Australian slang and rubbed her stomach. "You're making me hungry, mate."

"Oh, my Zeus." Ma fanned her face with her magazine. "You might want to control that in public, dear."

Oh. My. God. Ma seriously thought Winnie was talking about bodily functions, when ripper really meant something great. A winner.

Winnie looked confused, then shrugged. "I can't wait to see what he puts on the barbie. Should be tasty."

Ma was already shaking her head. "Kosmos no have barbies." She leaned toward Winnie with a devilish grin. "Trust me, he's all man. You stop by later. I give to you."

I slapped a hand to my forehead. Barbie meant grill or barbecue. I'd picked up enough Australian slang in the movies I'd seen and books I'd read. Apparently, Ma had not.

Winnie's eyes widened, then squinted in confusion. Again, she just shrugged and nodded her consent.

"Good girl." Ma picked up another magazine. "Speaking of bad girls. That woman is a menace. She thinks she's so much better than me. Who does she think she is, this *Ruby*?" Ma snorted. "I bet she changed her name to a jewel herself." She snapped the magazine and flipped the page.

"Don't let her get to you, 'Phelia," Aunt Tasoula said as she finished trimming Nik's cousin Thalia's hair. "*You're* Kalli's mama. *She's* nothing." Aunt Tasoula wrinkled her brow as if thinking. "It's crazy how much Kalli looks like her, though. Great skin, no wrinkles. I wonder what skin care routine she uses. Maybe I'll ask..."

Ma glared at my aunt.

My aunt wisely snapped back to attention.

"Wrinkles schminkles," she continued. "I see more of you in our Kalliope. It's true. You both have big eyes." She frowned. "Yours are extra big as they stare at me right now." She looked to me with wide eyes that screamed help. "You see what I mean, no?"

I blinked. Now how in the world did I answer that one? "I, um, definitely clean like Ma. My house is as spotless as her restaurant." That much was true, at least.

Ma sat a little straighter. "That's right. I teach you well."

Or I was born that way, I wanted to say but pressed my lips together and nodded.

"There's more to being a good woman than just looks. Ask Pop what kind of woman I am. He will tell you *very* good."

"You're a ripper, too," Winnie added.

"I beg your pardon, I would never. There's no ripping in my bedroom."

Winnie's face fell.

"Okay, maybe a little ripping. My Amos is the king of the rippers, but he's a man." Ma held up her hands. "What can you do?"

Everyone laughed, Aunt Tasoula like a hyena, and the tension was broken.

"Tasoula's right, Mrs. Ballas. DNA doesn't make someone a mother. You've been there for all of the important moments," Thalia seconded, eying my aunt's scissors.

Aunt Tasoula talked with her hands. That usually meant way more inches of hair clipped off than her customer was expecting. Her hands moved at a double-time pace after Ophelia's *look*. Some mothers had it down to a science, and Ma's look was enough to make even the most difficult child zip their lips, let alone a loose-lipped sister.

"That's good, Tasoula, thank you." Thalia hopped off the chair before my aunt could clip another strand and whipped off her cape.

"But...I no done."

"It's perfect just like this." Thalia ran a hand over her head, her smile slipping and eyes widening as she looked in the mirror. She swallowed hard at the strands of hair that were nearly spikes now. She looked like a punk rocker, her thick black hair not needing any gel to stand out in every direction.

"Well, I *am* pretty good." Aunt Tasoula smoothed a hand over her own hair and then waved her scissors about. "Opa! Who's next?"

"You're something, all right." Thalia stepped back.

Everyone else looked the other way.

Aunt Tasoula narrowed her eyes as her gaze scanned the room. "No haircut...no stay in shop."

Ma tossed her magazine down and walked over to sit in the chair.

"Smart woman." My aunt twirled the cape like a matador then wrapped it around my ma's shoulders with gusto and lifted her scissors.

Ma grabbed her hand. "Just my *normal* trim. Don't go getting all excited and messing up my hive, 'Soula. I'm watching you."

"Oh, woe is me, 'Phelia. You're such a worrywart." My aunt rolled her eyes but focused and started cutting at a much slower pace.

Thalia stepped closer to my ma and lowered her voice. "So, I was supposed to finalize a deal on a house for Richard and Fay Baker yesterday, but the deal fell through. The couple split up. Apparently, Fay found Ruby Winehouse in bed with Richard."

Aunt Tasoula gasped but didn't say a word, staying focused on what she clipped.

Ma grunted.

Thalia continued, "Ruby claimed the man never said he was married, so it wasn't her fault."

"You don't say." Ma's eyes widened. "That woman sure works fast. I know the Baker's. They come from money." She pursed her brow for a moment. "Richard is at least ten years younger than Ruby. She's a cheetah, that one."

"I think you mean cougar," I said.

"A cat's a cat. You know what I mean. She's a Mrs. Bobinson."

Aunt Tasoula nodded. "I think I know the Bobinsons. They have the diseases. Oh, our poor Kalli. What if she gets the cat scratch fever? She has the genes, you know."

"It means Ruby likes the young ones, you nitwit." Ma shook her head. "Kalli no get disease. Just keep trimming my hair."

"That's not all." Thalia leaned in even closer. "The Baker's found money missing from their dresser and accused Ruby of taking it, but she claims it wasn't her. Nik's looking into the matter. That woman really is a menace."

The door to Hera's Halo flew open, and in walked Mommy Dearest.

Murmurs rang out throughout the salon.

I groaned.

Her eyes settled on me. "Kalliope Mary Ballas, just the woman I wanted to see."

Obviously, she'd done her homework if she knew my full name.

"Over my dead body." Ma surged to her feet, Aunt Tasoula's cape billowing around her like some Greek mama superhero.

I held up a hand. "It's okay, Ma." She hesitated then finally sat back down and crossed her arms over her chest but kept her eyes firmly locked on Mommy Dearest.

My birth mother sashayed over to sit in the chair beside me, wearing black leather pants, a red skin-tight bodysuit that revealed her generous curves, her signature deep red lipstick and matching high heels. All I could think about was what horror I would have lived through if Ma hadn't adopted me. I shuddered.

I couldn't even think about what germs I might have encountered.

"That's quite a name you've got there," said the woman named *Ruby Winehouse*. She had no room to talk about *unique* names.

I struggled not to squirm, refusing to let her know she got to me, as I replied, "I'm rather fond of it."

I felt so awkward in the woman's presence. She hadn't made an effort to get to know me even once all week. We'd only exchanged a few words before I whisked Ma off to Doc's, and I hadn't seen the woman since.

Ruby eyed me from head to toe, lingering on my eyes. "I can't get over how much you look like me, sugar. It's like looking at myself nearly thirty years ago." She reached out and ran a finger down my suit-coat lapel. *So uptight and starched stiff, just like him.*

I flinched and leaned away from her touch. "Well, I wouldn't know about that."

She eyed me curiously. "About what, honey?"

"Who I look like." *Or acted like.*

"You look like me, but you obviously take after your father." She smacked her lips dryly, then fished her red lipstick out of her bra pocket and re-applied.

"I wouldn't know about that, either." I studied her, curious even though I didn't want to be.

"There's not much to know. He was in my life, and then he wasn't. Only spent one night together, but that's all it took. And look at you now. The best of both of us."

"I'm not anything of either of you." I crossed my arms uncomfortably. "What do you want, Ms. Winehouse?"

"Money," she blurted, confirming my suspicions. She lost the pretense of trying to be friendly, her face turning hard. "I've come upon some hard times, and you *are* my daughter, after all. You owe me."

My jaw fell open. The nerve of this virtual stranger. I clenched my teeth for a moment, trying to regain my composure. "I don't owe you anything, and

I'm *not* your daughter. It takes way more than an egg and a sperm to give either of you the right to call me that."

"All right, that's enough, Ruby Schmuby." Ma could read me like a book from clear across the room. She whipped off her cape and marched over to us.

Ruby stumbled to her feet, backing up toward the door, wise enough to understand you didn't mess with a Greek mama or her cubs.

"You leave *my* daughter alone, you hear me?" Ma poked her hard in the chest. "Or you no like the consequences."

"This isn't over." Ruby rubbed the red spot just beneath her collarbone. She backed away slowly, narrowing her eyes to slits as they settled on Ma, and glared menacingly at her with every step.

She didn't say a word, but it was clear she was thinking malicious thoughts.

Aunt Tasoula gasped after Ruby left. She grabbed a saltshaker she had nearby and threw some over her shoulder, then she spit.

"Did you just spit on me?" My cousin Eleni whipped her head around from her seat in the salon chair and gaped at Aunt Tasoula.

"Of course not." Aunt Tasoula's eyes shot left then right before she picked up a spray bottle. "New shine product. You love it. Trust me." She turned Eleni back around and blasted her with a shot for good measure then ran a comb through the mass.

Eleni didn't say anything more, but the doubtful frown remained on her face.

Ma faced Aunt Tasoula with an alarmed look. Their eyes met and an unspoken message passed between them.

Ma whispered, "Oh, no," and started ringing her hands.

Aunt Tasoula set the spray bottle down and replied gravely, "Oh, yes." She nodded and tsked.

"Oh, what?" I wondered what episode of the Twilight Zone we were in *this* time.

"Your mama is cursed!" Aunt Tasoula made the sign of the cross.

"Cursed how?" I was thoroughly confused.

Ma replied in barely more than a whisper, "Ruby Winehouse just gave me The Evil Eye."

CHAPTER 3

A week later, my biological mother still hadn't left town, putting a damper on my favorite time of year. The leaves were beginning to change, painting the town with deep orange, yellow, burgundy, and red. The colors were so crisp and vibrant, the air so fresh.

I couldn't even enjoy it.

The Harvest Festival had started and was being held in the park. It was past all the storefronts at the end of Main Street. There was a playground for children, a fenced in dog park, and a pavilion with picnic tables for events. Craft tents and food tables were scattered about, with bobbing for apples, burlap sack races, wagon rides, music and dancing going on for entertainment.

Our local socialite, Fay Baker, was hosting a charity auction with a fellow socialite, Elouise Sinclaire. Elouise wasn't from Clearview, but they ran in the same social circles across the tri-county area and often put on events together.

Mayor Riboldazzi had hired a handyman named Jasper Kent to help with whatever needed getting done. He had dark hair, green eyes and a muscular build. He was tan, but I didn't think he was Greek. Nik's cousin Thalia and my cousin Eleni were both arguing over who called dibs on him first. I couldn't blame them. Our town was small, and handsome strangers didn't come along too often.

My pop Amos and Papou Homer were putting the finishing touches on the table for Aphrodite's restaurant, while my cousins Kosmos and Silas were finishing the table for their deli, Diner Delights. My cousin Yanni was selling dried floral crafts at his Yanni's Yards landscaping table.

Meanwhile, YiaYia Dido was chasing Frona as she bounced past the finish line in her burlap sack, right past the winner's circle, hopping and singing her way towards the woods. Eleni and Thalia were bobbing for apples, while Ma, Aunt Tasoula, and Chloe were waiting to take a wagon ride.

Ma had never been very patient. She kept playing with the latch that lowered the gate in the back, waiting for the driver to let them climb aboard. Moments later the tailgate fell open with a loud bang, and the horses took off at a breakneck speed. Farmer Abbott flipped over the front seat into the wagon bed, cursing and struggling to climb back into his seat and regain control while Jasper jumped aboard to help him.

Everyone glared at Ma.

Aunt Tasoula spit.

Chloe clutched her Evil Eye Charm.

Nik and I wisely kept our distance as we waited for Boomer and Jaz to drop their dogs, Chanel and Versace, off to play in the dog park with Wolfgang. Dog walker Millie Donovan and her new boyfriend Nelson Rockwell of Rockwell Jewelers were volunteering for dog duty, so we could all take part in the festivities. The Fall Festival was one of my favorites, but Mommy Dearest had put a damper on everyone's mood.

"Sorry, we're late," Jaz said as she and Boomer joined Nik and me.

"Trust me, you didn't miss much except for Ma breaking Farmer Abbott's wagon." I winced.

"Really?" Jaz's lips parted. "She's still having bad luck?"

I nodded. "It's actually getting worse."

"Hey, Matheson, what happened to make you late?" Nik clapped Boomer on the shoulder.

"Salvatore Stallone called, saying he'd been robbed," Detective Matheson said with a weary tone, looking exhausted. His auburn hair was disheveled, and his clothes were wrinkled, but Jaz didn't seem to care one bit. She hung on his every word, standing arm and arm with him, looking picture perfect in every way.

Nik turned into detective mode in a flash. "Let me guess. It has something to do with Ruby Winehouse?"

"Bingo. What doesn't have to do with that woman? Since she came to town a couple weeks ago, we've had one report after another, filing complaints against her. This is the latest."

"Poor Mr. Stallone. What happened?" I wondered what more trouble the woman could possibly cause.

"Ruby came into Sal's Supermarket and walked around suspiciously for an hour, then she left. He checked the health and beauty aisle where she'd been lingering the longest against his inventory and noticed several items missing. He tracked her down at the Clearview Motel and confronted her, demanding she return the items she shoplifted."

"Interesting. She did tell me she was down on her

luck when she asked me for money at my aunt's hair salon," I said, and then asked, "How did she respond to Sal's accusations and demands?"

"She refused to give anything back, of course, claiming she didn't steal anything in the first place." Boomer scrubbed a hand through his hair, his eyes looking sleep deprived, making me wonder if his exhaustion had more to do with his new roommate and her pack than the case. "She refused to let him search her room, so he called the police station. By the time I got a warrant and arrived at the hotel, whatever she might have had was long gone."

"They got into a huge argument, with Sal threatening her if she ever stepped foot in his grocery store again, and vowing to get even with her," Jaz said. "I was in the car with our babies because I couldn't leave them alone. We were waiting on Daddy, so we could meet you guys here. Ruby and Sal were both shouting. I overheard everything."

Nik and I exchanged a glance. I didn't need to read his mind to know it meant, *See what I mean?* I might have to have a little talk with my love struck, baby fever, best friend who just a little while ago had been anti-relationship. To go from that to playing house with everything all at once had to have poor Boomer's head spinning.

"What about surveillance tapes? I'm sure Sal has them installed in his grocery store." Nik steered the conversation back on track.

"Already checked those out. They weren't at the right angle, so there's no proof she took anything. But with the festival going on, there weren't many people shopping at that time. Still, he can't prove the items didn't go missing at another time."

Nik pursed his brow. "Ruby's no amateur by the sounds of it."

"You have no idea," I said. "Ma thinks Ruby gave her The Evil Eye, so she's been wearing Evil Eye Charm necklaces, earrings, rings and bracelets. She cleaned out Rockwell Jewelers. Poor Nelson had to put in a rush order since half the town is Greek. They're now all paranoid and demanding more inventory."

"Isn't there something that's supposed to work to get rid of the curse? I think it's some special incantation passed down through generations, and you say it three times if I remember right," Nik said.

"Yes, the Xematiasma ritual. The incantation is top secret and only special people can perform it. Ma said she went to our Greek Orthodox Church and had it done by Father Papadopoulos, but she claims it didn't work." I shrugged.

"Oh, boy, no wonder she's a mess," Jaz said.

"They told her people with green eyes can transmit the curse stronger, and Ruby has green eyes. Ma's worried I'll become like my biological mother if I get too close to her, so she's become even more protective of me than normal. So basically, Ma's still getting headaches, bad luck, and driving everyone crazy."

"My ma believes in that superstition, too, but I don't," Nik responded.

"Maybe it's your non-Greek half, because I don't believe in it, either, but the rest of my family sure does. If Aunt Tasoula tries to throw salt over my shoulder and spit on me one more time, I'm going to lose it. Do you know how many germs are in someone's saliva?" I shuddered just thinking about it.

"Speaking of the troublemaker, she's here," Jaz said.

"Where?" I asked.

Jaz pointed to my pop's food table.

I looked over and I groaned. "That's not going to end well."

We all started walking in that direction at a quick pace.

Ruby bit into a sample of Fava—a dip similar to hummus, but made of yellow split pea, with a distinctive taste—and pita chips. She licked her lips sensually and rolled her green eyes dramatically. "Oh, Poppy, this is so delicious." She ran her finger down the front of his shirt, and his eyes bugged. "You're good." She leaned closer. "I'm sure you're a good man, too. You wouldn't want to see your poor daughter's mother hurting, would you?"

"You'll be hurting, all right, when his poor daughter's *mama* shoves her foot—"

"Ma!" I said, winded, coming to a stop between her and Ruby. "Don't do anything you're going to regret."

"Ha!" Ma leaned around me and pointed at Mommy Dearest. "She tried to steal *my* man, and *my* daughter. This one's going to regret the day she ever cursed me."

"Cursed? I think you wound your hair too tight in that nest of yours." Ruby stared at her as if she'd sprouted Medusa's snakes in her hive. "And you think I'm the crazy one." She snorted. "Trust me, darling, I don't have to steal *any* man, and I don't want *your* daughter. I made that clear decades ago."

I gasped, but she ignored me.

"You know what I want. I should be compensated for the gift I gave you. Give me what I want, and I'll go away. It's as simple as that."

Aunt Tasoula stepped out from behind Ma and threw salt over her shoulder. Chloe ducked, and then my aunt held her Evil Eye Charm in front of her as if it were a cross in front of a vampire. "Be gone, you witch! And your little curse, too. This isn't Kansas. You no belong here. Take the broom you came in on and fly away." She hacked a goober and then spit.

I threw up in my mouth a little.

Ruby hopped back just in time. "You're even crazier than your sister." She looked Ma in the eyes. "You know where I'll be." Then she turned around and left the festival.

"Oh, my aching head." Ma rubbed her duct taped temples. "Aloe didn't work and neither did your pop's duct tape. I have to do something. I don't know how much longer I can live with this curse." She walked away.

"It's true." Aunt Tasoula nodded. "Our YiaYia Maria was cursed with The Evil Eye. Poor YiaYia Maria had such bad luck, she fell in the barn and was kicked in the head by a mule. She went cross-eyed so bad, Dido had to run from side to side for her own ma to see her. And woe is me, the lump in the middle of her forehead looked like a unicorn, Zeus rest her sparkly soul." My aunt made the sign of the cross. "She had the bibopsy on it, and the news was grave. She was gone in six months. The Evil Eye is nothing to mess around with."

Lightning streaked across the sky and moments later, a boom of thunder shook the ground. Aunt Tasoula spit at me, tossed more salt, and went running to find Ma. I looked down at my slimy shoe and gagged. This time I wasn't so lucky.

I suddenly had a strong feeling that the worst of Ma's bad luck was yet to come.

～

"WHAT A DAY," I said to Nik as he sat at my kitchen table. It was almost one in the morning. We'd stayed until the festival closed, then headed home, and then I had to clean myself up, which took longer, given the spit germs.

Nik had to be the most patient man on the planet.

He looked so good in his blue cable knit sweater that matched his eyes and tapered dark blue jeans that fit him so well. It was hard not to stare at the muscles clearly evident beneath. He wore trendy blue plaid socks, but the smart man knew enough to leave his gray suede loafers at the door. He hadn't gone home to change into comfy clothes while I showered, probably afraid I wouldn't let him back in if he did.

I had to give it to him. He was stepping up his game and trying to impress me. Date number three had gone much better than two until Ma broke the wagon, Mommy Dearest flirted with Pop, and Aunt Tasoula spit on my shoes. I popped a beer and handed it to Nik then opened a bottle of chardonnay for myself and poured a hefty glass.

"Thanks." He took a long drink as I sat down across from him.

I'd changed into comfy clean yoga pants and a soft lilac fleece with matching socks the second I got home, of course. No amount of washing would get the germs out of my shoes to my satisfaction, so I'd thrown them out.

"I'm getting worried." I swirled the golden liquid around in my glass.

"Why?" He eyed me curiously.

"Our Greek families are crazy enough." I laughed a little too loud. "I don't need this new drama in my life right now."

His gaze softened. "Does it bother you that your biological mother is in town after all these years?"

"No...yes...I don't know." My shoulders slumped. "I really don't know how to feel about Ruby Winehouse. I used to have so many questions about who my birth parents were, and who I might look like, and why they gave me up, and why I'm the way I am?" I swallowed my lump of frustration, refusing to get emotional.

He waited silently until I was ready to continue.

"But this *stranger* has only confused me more. She doesn't have regrets or want to get to know me. She only wants money and to bank on my success. I refuse to do that. The problem is, Ma will do anything to make the woman go away. I know she feels threatened by her, but she shouldn't. Ma is my mother and always will be."

"Have you told Ophelia that?"

"Not in so many words." I twisted my lips and couldn't quite meet his eyes. "I have a hard time expressing my feelings."

"Really, you? I had no clue." He smirked.

"Ha ha. Very funny. Seriously, though, the only thing I've gained out of meeting my biological mother is knowing that I look just like her. Obviously, I didn't get my quirks from her, and I know nothing of my father. It would have been nice to meet someone who might actually *understand* what it's like to be me, but it doesn't look like that will happen anytime soon. I doubt I'll ever meet the man."

"Hey, you never know." He reached out and held my hand. "You might meet your biological father someday and discover the answers you're looking for. You certainly never imagined you would meet your biological mother. Maybe he'll be better than her. A little more caring. In the meantime, you have me." Nik pulled me onto his lap and held me in his arms as he lowered his head to kiss me.

My initial instinct to pull away made me stiffen, thinking of possible germs that might be entering my body at this very moment. But then his thoughts obliterated mine, allowing me to melt into him and just enjoy the moment. *I might not understand what it's like to be you, but I'm here for you always, baby. No one's perfect, but you're perfect for me. Oh, God, your lips are as sweet as honey. I think I'm falling in....*

Air whizzed by my head, and the world spun as I summersaulted off his lap. "Owww," I yelped from my perch on the floor.

"Are you all right?" Nik looked at me with wide eyes. "I'm so sorry. I don't know how that happened. Did I drop you or push you? How did you fall off my lap?"

"Nope, just clumsy ole' me."

I scrambled back onto my *own* chair, thank you very much. I adored Nik, but to hear him almost profess his love for me was too much to handle with everything else going on. I felt newfound empathy for Boomer.

Nik might not be pressuring me, but his thoughts sure were.

"Kalli, did I do something wrong?" He was a smart man and was starting to know me too well.

"I promise you, it's not you, it's me."

"Oh, God. That is never a good start to a conversation."

"It's not what you think?"

"And that's not much better."

Suddenly my phone started ringing, and I'd never been happier to hear from my ma. I quickly answered. "Hi, Ma, what's up?"

"K-Kalli?" Ma gasped; her voice shaky.

"Ma, it's okay, I'm here. What's wrong?" I looked at Nik who was in full Detective Steven's mode now, judging by his intense expression.

"I don't know what happened. I did everything she asked."

"Who?"

"Ruby Winehouse."

"What about Ruby? Ma, you're not making any sense. Where are you, and what happened?"

"I'm at the park, and the wicked witch is dead."

My heart dropped to the floor. Nik was already grabbing his keys and heading for the door. I was hot on his heels.

"Oh, Ma, what did you do?" was the last thing I said to her before her phone went dead.

CHAPTER 4

Nik and I pulled into the park where the Harvest Festival was being held. It was one in the morning, and everything had shut down for the evening at eleven. Ma's car was nowhere to be found, and neither was Ruby's rental.

A gust of wind swirled a pile of fallen leaves into a mini tornado across the parking lot. Suddenly, we saw a shadow peek from behind a tree then come running around front towards us, arms flapping like a blue herring trying to take flight. I didn't have to see the face.

That *had* to be Ma.

"Oh, thank Zeus it's only you," Ma cried out as she met us halfway. "I didn't do anything. I swear on Aphrodite herself."

"I'm still confused." I hugged her. *Am I sorry the witch is dead? Not so much.* I let go before I heard anything I couldn't unhear in the eyes of the law.

"Can you tell us exactly what happened, Mrs. Ballas?" Detective Stevens was definitely back on duty and watching us both closely.

"No, I can't." Ma shrugged.

The detective narrowed his eyes.

"You come with me. I show you. Then you see."

Nik and I followed Ma past the food tables, craft tents, and the entertainment stage until we came to the back of the park where the sack races and wagon rides were held. She finally came to a stop.

"There! You see?" Ma pointed to the wagon she broke earlier that day.

Bradley Abbott of Abbott's Farm hadn't been too happy with Ma. Her fidgeting hands had ruined today's hayrides, but he'd repurposed the wagon to hold a huge supply of harvested pumpkins, squash, watermelons and gourds he was selling in the tent up front. He wasn't going to be any happier with her tomorrow after he saw the latch he'd rigged back up had come loose again, with the tailgate flipped down, and his crop lying in a huge bruised worthless heap on the ground.

"The only thing I see is your string of bad luck continues." I looked around at the wake of her destruction.

"I no do this." Ma gestured to the broken wagon and huge mess on the ground, her accent always growing thicker when she was riled up. "And I no bury the wicked witch. It's kar-mama coming back to bite her. That's a thing, you know. Your cousin Silas had it once. You think Greek mamas are bad. You don't want the kar-mama after you." Ma shook her head. "That one's a naughty boy, and his bad juju came right back around to hit him in the face. Really. Knocked his front tooth right out." Her face pinched as she looked at the base of the mess and pointed. "And *that* one is pure evil."

I looked closer and sucked in a sharp breath as I saw an unmistakable pair of ruby red slippers sticking out from beneath the vegetable-slide. "Is she...?"

"I know nothing, I swear it." Ma threw her hands up in the air. "She was this way when I got here."

"Did you call Pop?"

"The man sleeps like the dead." She made the sign of the cross. "I call you right away. You take care of your mama like a good girl. No kar-mama for you."

Nik was on the ground, digging Ruby Winehouse out and checking for a pulse. I could hear the sirens wailing. He'd called 911 the moment he saw a body. All sorts of emergency vehicles covered the park now. The body was confirmed deceased, but she wouldn't be taken to the coroner's office until the CSI team finished processing the scene.

"What are you thinking." Detective Matheson walked up to Nik and surveyed the scene before him.

"I'm not sure yet." Nik looked at Ma and studied her. "Tell me everything you do know, Mrs. Ballas."

Ma sighed. "Everyone saw Crazy Lady argue with me before she left the festival. She was never gonna stay out of our lives unless I give her what she ask for. So, I call her hotel and told her I pay. She ask for five thousand dollars. I say I double the money, but this is one-time offer. She no step foot in Clearview and no contact ever again. She agree and tell me to meet her at park at midnight. Way out back. I think she really is a witch." Ma glanced at the body with a frown. "Or was."

Nik jotted down some notes. "Where's your car?"

"We both park down the street so we no look suspicious. I mean, who goes to the park this late?"

"If you were supposed to meet her at midnight, then why did you wait until one to call us?"

"It's the curse, I tell you. I wait for Amos to fall asleep, then I sneak out. Of course, my tire goes poof. My husband's gonna kill me. I no change tire. Never learned and never wanted to. I do enough." She swiped her hand through the air. "Anyway, I go so slow, but I was driving on the metal thingy and forty-five minutes late. By the time I walk to back of park, it was one. I thought she no show at first, but then I see those crazy shoes. I screamed then I call you. End of story." She wiped her hands clean of it. "It's a freak accident."

Boomer inspected the latch on the wagon and frowned. "Bradley Abbott rigged this up pretty good to make sure it held his harvest. I saw him do it myself. There's no way this came loose on its own. Someone had to tamper with it." He looked her in the eye. "Like you did earlier today."

Ma's jaw fell open. "Ruby got here before me. She could have played with the latch while waiting for me. I no the only one who fidgets."

Nik stood and joined Boomer. "I hate to say this, Mrs. Ballas, but Ruby was at the festival when you broke the wagon the first time. She wouldn't have touched the latch, knowing it was faulty. Like Detective Matheson said, it wouldn't have come loose on its own."

"If I wanted to kill her, why would I have brought money to pay her off?" Ma emptied her purse out on the ground and a wad of cash fell out. "See? Bribe money."

"Oh, Ma." I bent down and picked up the money. "I told you bribery never works. People like Ruby Winehouse would just keep coming back for more."

"Maybe she said something to that effect," Boomer speculated. "You realized the only way to make her stay out of your lives for good was to kill her and make it look like an accident."

"Are you accusing me of murder?" Ma's voice

raised two octaves as she pointed a finger in his face. "Boomer Matheson, wait until I talk to your mama. She no gonna be happy with you."

"No, ma'am." He squirmed uncomfortably. "I'm just trying to bring up all the possible arguments a prosecutor might point out, that's all, ma'am."

Ma's face flushed crimson. "Am I getting arrested? Oh, woe is me, the scandal. Amos no gonna like this."

"No one's accusing you of murder or arresting you. We're just trying to figure out what happened and find a way to clear your name. If someone tampered with the latch, and you got here late, then someone was here before you. The first thing we need to do is clear you, so we can focus on other suspects. Did anyone see you when you got the flat tire?" Nik asked.

"I snuck out, remember? I took the back roads to be sure I *wasn't* seen."

"I'm not saying I don't believe you." Boomer held his hands up before him. "All I'm saying is there's no way to prove you didn't get here at midnight, cause the accident when Ruby joined you, then wait an hour to be sure she was dead before calling us. You had motive and means and no alibi."

"It's not looking good, Ophelia," Nik added.

She narrowed her eyes. "Are you calling me a liar?"

"I would never," Nik wisely said.

Ma's face paled. "Then what does that mean?"

"It means the last of your luck just ran out, Ma."

THE NEWS that Ma was the number one suspect in the death of my biological mother had spread all over town before the next morning. Days later, the evidence was still only circumstantial. They didn't have any hard evidence to arrest and charge Ma with, so they'd let her go with firm instructions not to leave town and to stay out of trouble.

Nik wasn't on Ma's or his own mama's good list at the moment.

He tried to explain he was only doing his job, but they firmly told him a fourth date with me was on hold unless he proved Ma's innocence. At least the pressure to make us *official* was off for the moment, which wasn't a bad thing.

I needed to focus on clearing Ma's name.

The police had dusted the wagon latch for prints, but it was evident it had been wiped clean. Nik and Boomer both knew Ma wasn't a murderer, but they had to follow the law, especially if they wanted to prove to everyone else beyond a shadow of doubt that she was innocent. The body had been sent to the coroner, Mable Griffith, for an autopsy to be performed to determine the cause of death and time.

I didn't know how I felt about Ruby dying, other than I felt guilty for feeling indifferent. Yes, she was my biological mother, but for all intents and purposes she was a stranger to me. The woman had done nothing but stir up trouble from the moment she arrived in town, not to mention demanding money from us.

And now my real mama was the only suspect in her death.

I needed to figure out who might want Ruby Winehouse dead from her own town of Cloudsville. Who might want her dead from Clearview as well. And possibly even who might want to set Ma up. Once I figured all of that out, I could start putting the pieces of the puzzle together. A couple days had already gone by, and time was ticking.

"I'm so hungry." Jaz stepped up to the counter.

We went to Diner Delights for lunch. My family ran half the businesses in town. At one point my cousins, Kosmos and Silas, were the only members of my family that Jaz got along with. Probably because they were young, single, attractive men . . . and off limits, which made them that much more appealing.

Just because we had an agreement that she couldn't date my family members did not mean that would stop her from flirting outrageously with them every chance she got. But now that she was official with Boomer, my family had warmed up to her.

Kosmos was on the short side but built like a tank. He kept his dark hair cropped tight, and it somehow matched his stature: tough as nails. But his eyes gave him away. They were the soft, dreamy, sleepy bedroom eyes that all women fell for, yet he was single. Although, I had seen Winnie hanging around more often.

Kosmos didn't seem to mind one bit.

Then there was Silas. He was the biggest flirt of our family. Thinner but taller, with thick curly black hair and dimples that worked their charm every time. He'd finally met his match in Flannigan's bartender, Zena Renner. She was a petite dynamo with pixie cut blonde hair, lavender eyes, a big smile, and a personality to match.

He'd been a goner the moment he'd laid eyes on her.

Kosmos stood behind the deli counter, making sandwiches. He gave us a friendly wave when we came in. Meanwhile, Silas ran the register. He shot me a quick grin and Jaz a wink. She laughed and blew them both kisses.

I just rolled my eyes.

"I don't have much of an appetite," I said.

"How is Aunt Ophelia?" Kosmos asked.

"She's one tough mama. Pop tried to ground her for the flat tire. You can imagine how well that went over. She's determined to prove her innocence no matter the cost, making Nik's job that much harder."

"I hear that. Boomer's been complaining for days because Ophelia and Tasoula are playing cops and robbers, showing up everywhere around town and interfering in the investigation." Jaz eyed the sandwiches. "I'll have a caprese sandwich, please."

"Ordering an Italian sandwich in a Greek deli is sacrilegious." Kosmos teased as he set to work on making it anyway.

"Are you sure you aren't part Italian?" Jaz teased back. "You make it so good."

"Bite your tongue, woman." Silas laughed as he rang her up.

"I'll have a Greek salad," I chimed in.

"Atta girl." Kosmos grinned.

"Suck up." Jaz shot me a mock scowl.

"I grew up Greek. What do you expect?" I paid Silas then we sat down at a table to eat.

For a moment, we ate in silence, the enticing aromas and delicious flavors putting us both in food heaven. The door to the diner opened once more, and in walked Wallace Newcomer and Mable Griffith. Wally's family had owned Newcomer's Funeral Home since before I was born, and Mable was our local coroner.

Wally went to high school with Ma and Aunt Tasoula, but Mable had only been in town for about five years. She was around their age but a petite thing. She had short brown hair, black slacks and a gray sweater. I'd always found her kind of quiet and shy whenever we'd spoken, which wasn't often.

Meanwhile, Wally towered over her.

They headed for the counter, but he spotted me first. Pausing, he bent way down to give Mable his order, and then he changed directions. She looked startled for a moment, then smiled shyly at us before stepping up to the counter.

"Hi, Kalli, how's your poor mother?" He gestured to the chair across from me in question, and I nodded so he sat down, pushing the small round glasses up his nose. He was tall and skinny, with thick brown wavy hair and milk chocolate brown eyes. He wore khaki pants and a tan sweater.

I was so tired of answering questions about my mother, but I understood. Everyone wanted to know on a daily basis how she was doing, being the only suspect in a murder case. Especially because the victim was my biological mother.

The whole situation was messy and complicated.

"Ma's being Ma. Stubborn as the day is long and won't listen to anyone's advice. She certainly won't stand for anyone telling her what to do when she knows she's right about something."

"I get it." He smiled a little and looked at me with sympathy. "I've known your mother for all of her life. She's not a killer."

"Oh, I know that. Ma might be very vocal about how she's feeling, but she would never actually harm anyone."

He shook his head, looking confused. "I can't believe the police think Ruby's death was murder and not just a freak accident. Who knows why Ruby was at the park that late at night? My mother always said nothing good happens after midnight."

"She was there to meet Ma."

His eyes widened. "Really? I hadn't heard that."

"Ma was there to pay Ruby off, even though I'd told her not to give her a cent."

His eyes filled with compassion and understanding. "Unfortunately, bribery never works."

"That's what I tried to tell her, but she's so stubborn, she didn't listen."

"You don't think your mother is guilty, do you?"

"No way. Ma was running almost an hour late. Someone was there before her. I won't stop looking until I figure out who." I blinked, not intending to reveal that much. Wally had a way of making people open up to him without even asking.

"Well, I'm here if you need anything at all." He squeezed my hand. *That poor family. What a mess.* "Don't hesitate to ask."

I relaxed over the sincerity ringing though his thoughts and his comment. "Thank you. That means a lot."

"Of course. I sure feel bad for your mother." He looked at me. "How are *you* holding up, given Ruby Winehouse was your biological mother?"

"Everyone keeps asking me that. Honestly, I don't know how to answer. The woman was a stranger to me. It did feel weird seeing a dead body that looked just like me. An older version of me, as if I were seeing my future." I shivered.

"I understand." His voice was full of warmth. He was born to be a funeral director: soft spoken, comforting, kind. "I came in for lunch, but I'm glad I ran into you. I wanted to talk with you about another matter that involves you."

"Me?" I felt a trickle of unease flow through my body and wondered if that could damage my cells.

"Yes. Coroner Griffith finished her autopsy report, and she's ready to release Ruby Winehouse's body to her next of kin." His gaze met and held mine.

"Okay, so what does that have to do with me?" I started to squirm. "I'm sure Ruby has some sort of relative around."

"Actually, she doesn't."

"I don't understand what you're getting at." I shot Jaz a look, worried I actually did understand and wasn't liking what I was about to hear.

"Well, my dear, you would now be her only living next of kin." He paused a tension-filled beat before adding, "The question is, what would you like to do with your mother's remains."

CHAPTER 5

I barely knew Mommy dearest, yet I was her next of kin. How was that possible that she had no other family? How was I supposed to know what to do with the remains of a virtual stranger? The coroner, Mable Griffith, released Ruby's body to me, so I had her brought to Newcomer Funeral Home. Ma wasn't too happy about that and not much help in what I should do with her.

Or at least her ideas weren't exactly appropriate.

I was thinking cremation. A funeral service was a lot more expensive, and I didn't have a clue what I would say about the woman. Cremation and a private ceremony—where I came to terms with meeting my biological mother and then losing her without really learning a thing about her—was more my speed. It wasn't like we'd ever talked about her wishes.

We'd barely talked at all.

As far as I could tell, she hadn't made a will or written her wishes down. Ma refused to let her share my plot, which I guess I couldn't blame her. Wally said he would hold Ruby's body until I made my decision.

We'd just come from Sunday mass at our Greek

Orthodox Church and were having brunch in my parents' back yard. Lights were strung all over the gazebo, with Greek statues and fountains gracing the yard, and enough food to feed a small army.

My family mixed with Nik's pretty much *was* a small army.

As we'd walked out of church, Agnes Georgiou—the choir director—said it was Ma's fault that she was cursed with The Evil Eye. That it never would have happened if she hadn't adopted the spawn of the devil in the first place.

Aunt Tasoula held Ma back from doing anything she might regret.

Chloe tried to defend her by saying, "Don't insult my future daughter-in-law."

Agnes replied, "Your son doesn't count either, because he's only *half* Greek."

Aunt Tasoula let go and joined Ma and Chloe as all three jumped Agnes in the parking lot. Pop, Papou, and Nikos all had to break it up. Father Papadopoulos was *not* happy. Let's just say none of them were welcome back into church until they learned how to behave.

I'd never been more embarrassed in my life.

"That woman has never liked me." Ma filled her plate a second time. "I feel like everyone is ganging up on me." She sniffled.

"What does she know." Pop kissed Ma's cheek. "She's just an uptight spinster and jealous because she no marry or have babies."

Ma patted his cheek. "You're a good egg, Amos."

"According to her, *my* baby is only half a man and doesn't count." Chloe pouted. "Just because his pop wasn't Greek doesn't make my Nikos flawed. His father was a blond-haired, blue-eyed Viking. He just wasn't a good husband."

Captain Crenshaw squeezed her shoulder. He smiled down at her, his steel gray eyes crinkling, looking distinguished with his salt and pepper hair. "Nik is part of you. Nothing that comes from you could possibly be flawed."

"Well, aren't you sweet. I'd say I got me a good egg too, Quincy." Chloe smiled up at him with dreamy eyes, and he winked at her. They'd only been on a few more dates than Nik and me, yet she'd agreed to be *official* pretty quickly.

Just another thing that irked Nik.

"Sweet on me, take a knee, ask the woman to marry thee." Frona sang and skipped circles around them, throwing handfuls of leaves in the air, her uneven pigtails bouncing with every step.

Quincy quirked a brow.

Chloe blushed.

Nik narrowed his eyes.

"Come on, Frona, help me get more cans of olives from the kitchen." YiaYia Dido dragged Frona away.

"Half a man, no understand, the answer's no, Devil's Spawn say so." Frona sang over her shoulder until she disappeared into the house.

I coughed.

Nik frowned.

Ma shook her head.

A streak of lightening zipped across the clear blue sky. Even the gods weren't happy with me. What more could possibly go wrong? Just then the heavens opened up, and it started to rain buckets on us. Everyone made a mad dash inside.

Ma handed out towels, and everyone congregated in the great room. My parents had a two-story colonial with fountains and statues out front as well. The cousins all brought the food inside while everyone talked about the Harvest Festival that was still going on.

I wandered closer to the sunroom in the back where I spotted Captain Crenshaw and Detective Stevens with their heads bent over a notebook. Nik was being very closed mouthed with me about the case.

I thought it might be because our Ma's had suggested we hold off dating until my Ma's name was cleared, and I had agreed, much to his dislike. He said it had nothing to do with that. It was because I was too close to the case, same as when the captain had pulled him from the last murder investigation because *his* ma was a suspect.

And just like him, I didn't plan to sit idly by and do nothing.

"Sounds good. Make sure you follow that lead," Captain Crenshaw said. "Any updates on Pearl?"

Who was Pearl? I stayed out of the sunroom but leaned against the wall and listened through the crack in the open door.

"Boomer and I drove over to Cloudsville and questioned the people Ruby worked with. Pearl wasn't too happy with Ruby when she left town without paying her the club's share of the cut from the last week she stripped at Pearl's Place."

Nik had told me he'd looked Ruby up when she first came to town, claiming to be Mommy Dearest, and that she was a stripper. Pearl must have been her boss. I made a mental note to add Pearl to my list of suspects.

"Some of the other strippers said Pearl got a tip that Ruby was headed to Clearview to find her daughter. Pearl claims she came to the festival because she heard it was great, and that's all."

"Ask around Clearview to see if any locals know anything more."

"Will do."

"Anything else from Cloudsville?" Captain asked.

"I guess one of the regulars at Pearl's Place was obsessed with Ruby. He asked her out on a weekly basis, and she always turned him down." I heard papers rustle. "His name's Grayson Millbrook. A powerful businessman with lots of money and connections who is used to getting his way. Let's just say he doesn't like to be told no."

Grayson Millbrook. That was another name I needed to add to my list of suspects.

"Does he have an alibi?"

"Says he drove to New York City on business overnight. I'm working on verifying his story, but even if he does have an alibi, he has plenty of questionable contacts who would gladly do him favors."

"I'm surprised Ruby didn't just take the man up on his offer. She said she needed money and seemed pretty desperate. He could have been her solution."

"Unless he's into things even scarier than she is, and she wanted no part of it. The man's a decent looking guy. There had to be a reason for her to say no to him. Something or someone had her spooked."

"What about here in Clearview? I know Ruby stirred up plenty of trouble the short time she was here."

"Boomer's looking into those leads. There's Salvatore Stallone who vowed to get even with her for shoplifting from his supermarket. Not to mention, Richard and Fay Baker. They were the *it* couple of

Clearview. He comes from money, and Ruby smelled that a mile away. That's why she seduced him."

"I heard Fay filed for divorce, which is a scandal to a family like the Bakers. They're all about their image and how society sees them. Even Elouise has kept her distance from Fay, and the charity auction is suffering."

"You heard right, but Richard is still trying to get Fay back. He also vowed to make Ruby pay for ruining his life, and Fay was heard saying she was happy Ruby was dead. That she got what was coming to her. Fay is focusing on restoring her image now that Ruby is gone."

"There's no scarier person than a scorned woman." The captain grunted.

"Except maybe a scorned Greek woman." Nik chuckled, and more papers rustled. "That's all I have so far."

"Well, except for Ophelia Ballas, of course," the Captain pointed out.

"That's true, though I don't think any of us believe she could be capable of killing anyone."

"She's a Greek mama. They're capable of just about anything when it comes to their children. I know the job can be difficult, but it doesn't matter what we think. We get paid to be objective and do our jobs. Can I count on you to do that?"

"Yes, sir."

"Kalli, what are you doing out here?" Chloe asked in a loud voice as she came up beside me.

Greek mamas were anything but quiet.

The door swung open fully, and Nik's gaze passed between his ma and myself, landing and narrowing on me. "I'd like to know the answer to that myself."

The front door to my parents' house suddenly burst open.

Wally stood, panting hard, as he searched the crowd until he saw me. He inhaled a deep breath and then blurted with a wince, "Your mother's missing."

"Wallace Newcomer, you're such a character," Ma said, shaking her head. "I'm standing right here."

"Not you, Ophelia," Wally replied with a serious look, his gaze glued to mine. "I'm talking about Ruby Winehouse. Her body has vanished."

"RUBY WAS RIGHT HERE, I swear it," Wally said, opening one of the refrigerated compartments that housed the corpses in the morgue in the back of his funeral home, which was clearly empty.

"Well, she's definitely not now." Detective Stevens made a note in his notebook. "Can you tell me what happened, Mr. Newcomer?"

"Please, call me Wally." He pushed his glasses back up his face, his dress shirt a wrinkled mess with sweat stains. "I really don't understand how she's missing." He scrubbed a hand through his hair while he paced. "I put her body in the refrigerator compartment to slow decomposition until Kalli decided what she wanted to do with her mother—"

Ma cleared her voice.

"—her biological egg donor's body," Wally quickly amended. "I checked on her this morning, then took a lunch break. When I came back, she was gone."

"Did you lock the door?" Detective Stevens asked.

"Yes, I always do, though I'm not sure why." Wally continued to pace. "I mean who actually *wants* to break into a funeral home?"

"Do you have any cameras?" I was determined to find out what happened. I felt a sense of responsibility as her only living relative, whether I liked it or not.

"I've never felt the need." Wally stopped pacing and looked at me with regret. "Most want nothing to do with a funeral home because they don't like talking about death, or being near death, knowing we have a morgue."

"You do charge a fee for your services, don't you?" Detective Stevens pointed out logically.

"Of course."

"Then there's always a possibility of break-ins. Desperate people will look anywhere for money."

"I suppose you're right, but most of our transactions are in the form of checks or paid digitally online," Wally said. "A couple drawers and filing cabinets were riffled through, but nothing was taken except for Ruby's body."

"Larry Miller said Ruby's room at the Clearview Motel was ransacked." Detective Stevens checked his notes. "Whoever took her was looking for something."

"Was anyone still here during your lunch break?" I asked.

"No, this is a small family operated business." Wally looked genuinely upset. "We all take lunch at the same time, never dreaming something like this would be a possibility. We're in the business of easing a family's grief, not adding to it."

"No worries there," Ma said on a snort.

"Ma!" I shot her a pleading look, and she just pursed her lips.

"Who else had a key or access to the building?" Detective Stevens walked around the room and studied everything from all angles.

"The cleaning crew and bookkeeper. That's about

it." Wally led us back into the main lobby with the reception desk and sitting area, which was tastefully decorated for comfort and elegance.

Detective Stevens peeked in other offices as we walked past and even the larger room where services were held.

"My poor daughter is being put through the wringer on this one. She shouldn't even have to be responsible for a woman who was never responsible for her," Ma said. "And now the body goes missing? How does that even happen with today's security? I know my daughter. She no relax until everything is right in her world." Ma thrust her finger in his direction. "You need to make this right, Wally."

Wally stopped and faced Ma with a heartfelt, sincere look in his eyes. "I promise you, Ophelia, I will do everything in my power to fix this. I feel so bad that you have to go through this. You are such a good person. You don't deserve anything you've been going through. Anyone who knows you, knows you couldn't possibly hurt anyone."

"Well, thank you, Wally, but I'm not the only one going through this. Kalli's the one who doesn't deserve any of this. She is an innocent victim in all of this. She was the one who was given up when she was born, only to meet her birth mother this way and then to have her murdered. I know I'm innocent, and the truth will prevail. What I want most is justice for my daughter. That's all."

"And you shall have it," Wally said. "I can promise you that."

CHAPTER 6

Looking around Jaz and Boomer's apartment as I sipped my glass of chardonnay, I finally chose a spot to sit. I curled up on the only comfy looking piece of furniture in the place. An over-stuffed leather couch in the living room. The guys were out chasing down leads, while Jaz and I were having a girls' night to catch up.

"I like your place," I said.

"Thanks. It's getting there. I still have a long way to go before it feels like home." Jaz sipped her apple martini.

She joined me on the other end of the couch, her full-size black poodles following her to lay in their custom-made, blinged-out designer dog beds. Chanel and Versace really were so well-behaved, but a lot of work nonetheless for someone who wasn't used to having pets around. I inhaled deep. The place smelled of Jaz.

Good taste and class.

The apartment was a three-bedroom townhouse and while it smelled like Jaz, it was totally a bachelor pad. The furniture was mismatched with gaming chairs and sports posters scattered around the living room.

Jaz and Boomer shared a bedroom, Chanell and Versace shared a bedroom, and the third bedroom was full of gym equipment. Jaz had started to sprinkle her flavor all over the place, but it didn't exactly mesh with Boomer's style.

"About that," I started.

Jaz frowned. "About what?"

"Making this place feel like home."

"What's wrong with that?"

"Nothing." I held up a hand. "Don't get me wrong. I am so happy for you and Boomer. Truly, I am."

"No offense, but I hate when people start conversations that way," Jaz pointed out. "You're my best friend, Kalli. Just give it to me straight."

"Boomer is crazy about you. I hope you know that."

"I do. So, what's the problem?"

I hesitated for a moment. "*You* are the problem." I bit my bottom lip.

She gaped at me. "Excuse me?"

"Hear me out. First you play hard to get and pretty much say you are against marriage and kids. Then when the poor guy finally wins you over, you do a complete one-eighty. His head has to be spinning, trying to keep up with you."

"Is he saying something to you?" Jaz's face paled. "Has he changed his mind? Oh, God, he has, hasn't he? He doesn't love me anymore and wants out."

"No and no. I'm not very good at talking about relationships, you know that. All I'm trying to say is that Boomer has been talking to Nik a little, and anyone with eyes can see he's exhausted and overwhelmed."

She snapped her spine straight and took a big sip

of her martini. "Well, he's the one who asked me to move in with him."

"Yes, he did. But I don't think he expected to suddenly be the proud papa of two diva dogs who are more like children. You have to admit, it's a lot. His place is being taken over by females."

"Well, maybe I should move out, then."

"Good Lord, that's not what I'm saying at all, Jaz. I'm sure Boomer wouldn't be happy with Nik or me if you moved out because of something we said." I reached out and squeezed her hand.

Great. Just when I finally let my guard down for a guy, he's going to hurt me.

I let go. "No, he's not going to hurt you."

"No fair with the mind reading thing."

"I'm just saying maybe don't bring the dogs everywhere you guys go. Ease into this with Boomer. He adores you. Anytime you live with someone, you have to compromise. It's about give and take to make it work. Look how long it took us to adjust to living together."

She relaxed back onto the couch. "That's true, and you're right. I kind of threw it all at him to see if he would leave me. I don't want him to. I'm just still so afraid a relationship won't work and will break my heart like my parents' failed relationship did to my dad."

"You and Boomer are not your parents. Just ease up a little and enjoy this next phase of your lives."

"Speaking of next phases. What about you and Nik? What's stopping you from making your relationship official? It's not like marriage, and you're not even moving in together. You're just agreeing to be exclusive with each other. Isn't that what you want? Or do you care if he dates other women."

"Of course, I don't want him to date other women." I inhaled a deep breath, held it, then slowly released it. "You and Boomer have known each other for years. I really like Nik, but we haven't known each other all that long. I guess I'm afraid he'll figure out I'm a freak, and I'll be devastated."

Her eyes softened as they held mine captive, refusing to let me run from this topic like I usually did. "You still haven't told him about your mind reading ability?"

"No." I held up my hand with my palm firmly facing her. "Before you say anything, I'm not ready to. He's the first man who doesn't care about my quirks." I took a big sip of my wine. "I just can't risk him thinking this ability is too much to handle, even though he doesn't realize it's the only way a relationship between us is even possible."

"Are you ever going to tell him?" Jaz asked softly.

"Someday, yes. Just not right now. Ma needs me."

"Good point. This probably wouldn't be the best time. I heard Ruby's body went missing. What kind of person does something like that?"

"I have no clue, but I feel like I'm living in an alternate universe where Clearview and its residents are the same yet completely different."

"I know, it's like something right out of a movie. I've never seen Sal get so mad over a shoplifter. Then the Bakers, who were the *it* couple, break up. Agnes causes total chaos at church, and now Wally loses a body. What the heck is happening to our town?"

"Ruby Winehouse is what happened, and now I'm stuck cleaning up her mess."

"I'm so sorry you're going through this."

"Me, too."

"How's the case going, anyway?"

"Not good. The festival is still going on. Mayor Riboldazzi is pushing for the case to be closed quickly because Clearview needs the revenue from the festival. It's all becoming a lot to deal with, making my anxiety worse than ever."

"How are you stuck cleaning up her mess? You don't owe her anything. It's really not fair."

"I'm not doing it for her. I'm worried Ma will do something stupid to clear her name. And when you get Aunt Tasoula as her sidekick, all sorts of trouble happens."

My cell rang, and I looked at the caller ID.

"Who is it?" Jaz asked.

"Nik," I said and frowned. What on earth was he doing calling me this late? "Hey, you. I didn't expect to hear from you because, well, you know." I cleared my throat. Putting dating on hold made everything so awkward between us, which was the last thing I'd wanted. "Is something wrong?" I listened to him talk, and the color drained from my face. "Do you want me to come get her?" My gaze met Jaz's, and I shook my head. "Are you sure you have it covered?" My shock gave way to frustration. "Okay, thank you. I really appreciate it." I hung up.

Jaz quirked a brow. "What was that about?"

I sighed. "Trouble."

~

TROUBLE, of course, was Ma.

We were going to have to get her a change-of-name form if she didn't stop causing disturbances all over town. We were all at the Harvest Festival, trying to support our town and, well, keep Ma in line.

"Ma, you can't keep stirring up trouble." I tightened my sweater. The fall weather was growing colder every day.

We walked by Vincenzo Ricci's table full of samples from his Italian restaurant. He glared at Ma, gesturing in what I was sure was not a flattering compliment to her. She brushed him off with a gesture of her own and kept walking.

"I no stir up trouble. I wait until closing time to have the talk last night. I can't help it the man is a hothead. Steam was shooting out his ears like the old coal trains."

"You accused him of tampering with the latch on the wagon to set you up so the whole town would think you were the one who killed Ruby."

"Well...he *could* have done it. That's all I say. He was one of the last people to leave the festival, and he drives right by the park on his way home. I can't help it Aphrodite's beats Vincenzo's every year in the A Tast of Clearview contest. What can I say? I'm a better cook. He's a man. He can't handle that."

"You're lucky he didn't press charges."

"I no do anything wrong. I talk, that's all."

"And you refused to leave until he admitted what he did, which he refused to do because he says he didn't do it. I know you want to figure out what happened to Ruby so you can prove your innocence, but causing more trouble is not helping."

Last night, Nik had known I'd needed a girls' night desperately. When he'd called, he'd told me to stay at Jaz's. That he could handle Ma. He had already calmed Vinny down and brought Ma home with no charges filed. He'd just wanted to keep me in the loop. I hadn't seen him yet today, but he'd said he would be here. Something about helping the festival out.

"Bah." Ma brushed me off and kept walking toward the back of the park by the entertainment stage. "You sound like your pop."

"Well, maybe you should start listening to us."

"Speaking of Pop, there he is." Ma ignored my comment and headed in his direction with a proud, confident step to her gait.

He was standing by Papou, YiaYia, and Frona in the growing crowd in front of the stage. My cousin Eleni and Nik's cousin Thalia were front and center. Silas and Zoe were together by Jaz and Boomer as well as Chloe and the captain by Aunt Tasoula.

"What's going on?" I asked Jaz when we reached them.

"The bachelor auction." She grinned at me and winked at Boomer.

"No bidding for you," he teased.

"I wouldn't dream of it." She hugged him. "I already won the bachelor I wanted months ago."

"No Chanel and Versace?" I looked around and smiled on the inside. Looked like she took my advice.

"Not today. It's a date night for me and my man."

Boomer smiled down at her with a besotted look.

My heart warmed, and I looked around. Now, to find *my* man. I blinked. Or my whatever we were calling ourselves. I didn't see him anywhere and was about to text him when Mayor Riboldazzi took the mic.

"Ladies and gentlemen, we have a special surprise for you tonight. Some of Clearview's finest bachelors up for auction. When I open this curtain, we'll start the bidding. There will be a winner for each gentleman, and the winner will be treated to a date with the fellow she wins." With great gusto, he pulled back the curtain.

I gasped, and my mouth fell open wide, my heart dropping to my stomach.

Nik's eyes locked onto mine, and he grinned.

Anger overrode my shock. "What is he doing up there?" I ground out.

"He *is* single," Boomer pointed out. "Besides, it's for a good cause."

"Why don't you bid on him," Jaz said all innocent like. "You heard Boomer. It's for a good cause."

"That's one underhanded way to get me to go on another date with him," I muttered more to myself.

"*If* you win the bid, Cuz," Silas said, having obviously overheard us. "Looks to me like there are plenty of women who would kill for a chance to date Detective Stevens."

I frowned. *Not on my watch.*

Nik was the first one up. I raised my paddle immediately, and so did half the crowd. Ugh.

"Do I hear one hundred dollars?"

The group of bidders went down by a third.

"Do I hear five hundred dollars?"

The group of bidders went down to half.

"Do I hear one thousand dollars?"

Anastasia Stewert, Jaz's rival and owner of Vixen boutique, raised her paddle sky high.

"Going once, going twice, going—"

"Five thousand dollars!" I waved my hand through the air like a lunatic fending off a swarm of killer bees.

The crowd hushed, and everyone gaped at me.

"But the last bid was only at one thousand." Mayor Riboldazzi stared at me, his expression thoroughly confused.

"And now it's at five thousand. Going once, going twice, sold!" I said and tossed my paddle to a gaping Anastatia as I strode past her and held out my hand to

Nik, not about to let anyone else claim my man. "Come on, Detective, you can get down now."

He quirked a brow.

"Please," I added, feeling my cheeks heat.

"Is that your official decision?"

"An official date, yes. Don't push your luck for anything else."

He climbed down and slowly walked over to me, taking my hand in his. "Deal." *It's a start.*

"It's a *date*," I clarified, even though he didn't know I'd heard his thoughts, adding, "if you still want me."

He leaned down and kissed me as an answer. *You have no idea just how much.*

The crowd cheered but all I heard were his thoughts...until I felt a set of eyes on me. I scanned the crowd, but there were so many people from out of town, it was hard to pinpoint who might be a threat.

"Well, folks, we still have a stage full of eligible bachelors just waiting to sweep you off your feet."

The mayor started the bid for the next man. Winnie Wallaby won a date with my cousin Kosmos, and Ma let out an opa! Coroner Mable Griffith won a date with Wallace Newcomer, but everyone knew they were only best friends. Eleni and Thalia fought hard over Jasper, but Thalia made more money than Eleni as a realtor and ended up winning.

The last man stood on the stage.

Tate Hemsworth of Hemsworth Hardware went to high school with Ma and Aunt Tasoula and Wally. Ma had lived in Clearview all her life while Pop's family moved to Clearview right after graduation.

Tate looked like a big blond blue-eyed Viking.

All I could think is this must be what Nik's father looks like. I'd met Tate before at his store, but I didn't really know him that well. He was divorced, with five daughters and several grandkids.

Even I had to admit he was still one good-looking man.

Tate's gaze landed on Ma and held for a moment. Pop stood a little straighter and slipped his arm around her. Ma patted Pop's hand, and Tate bowed his head slightly before looking away.

Once again, Mayor Riboldazzi opened the bidding. Bids from women older than him as well as his age came in. He even received bids from women half his age.

"Sold!" I heard, jarring me from my thoughts.

"Tasoula! How could you?" Ma said after Pop had gone back to man the Aphrodite's table.

"How could I not? Look at him." Aunt Tasoula waved to Tate who raised a brow and waved back, his smile growing broader.

"You no hear of girl code?" Ma crossed her arms over her ample chest.

"It's been over forty years, Ophelia. Girl code has expired. Past its prime. More like withered up and died."

"Are you saying I'm old?" Ma growled.

"I no say you old. I say girl code is old."

"I'm on to you. You think I'm no fun anymore."

Tasoula flipped her hair over her shoulder. "If the wrinkle fits."

"Wrinkle Schminkle. Just because I no use all those crazy masks like you. You look like an alien in those."

"Ah, but they work, 'Phelia. You come to my salon. I show you."

"And I show *you*!" Ma lunged for her.

I stepped between them. "Ma, stop." I looked her

in the eyes, a little worried. "What do you mean girl code?"

She heaved out a sigh. "Your Pop wasn't my first love." She paused a minute and let that sink in. "Tate was. We dated during our senior year and went to prom together. I was a real looker back then."

My heart did a funny little flip. "D-Do you still love him?"

"Of course not, honey." She held my cheeks, and I could feel her sincerity. "I love your pop. *He* is the man for me." She kissed my forehead and then let me go.

"Tate wasn't Greek," Aunt Tasoula said, "so your mama could no marry him."

"I no regret dating Tate, but the moment I met Amos, I knew he was the man for me." Ma's eyes hardened. "That no mean I want my younger sister to marry my ex-boyfriend. Find a nice Greek man, 'Soula."

"I'm widowed, not dead, Ophelia, and I no look for a husband." Aunt Tasoula winked at me. "It's only one date. Tate might not be Greek, but he *is* a god. Excuse me, ladies. I gonna have me some fun." She scurried off to Tate, her hips swinging more than normal every step of the way.

"That woman gonna give me the migraine yet." Ma huffed off to join Pop.

I rubbed my aching temples, knowing exactly how she felt. This day was getting stranger by the minute. The problem was, there were a lot of hours left in this day, and something told me there were stranger things to come.

CHAPTER 7

That evening Nik and I went to Rosalita's Place for our date. Rosalita's was a Mexican restaurant on the outskirts of town. One of the few places not owned by a member of my family or Nik's. I went to high school with Rosalita, and I knew her kitchen was clean.

That was the only reason I could eat here.

I still brought my own utensils in my purse, much to the amusement of my date. I had pulled them out and arranged them on my sanitized napkin three times when we first arrived, and I kept fidgeting with them now.

We'd just finished dinner and were eating dessert.

"You all good now?" Nik's lips twitched with his effort not to smile.

"Yes, in fact, I am." I smirked, then pointed out my logic. "Rosalita is a clean freak, but I can't be certain all her employees abide by her rules. Heating water to 145 degrees Fahrenheit might purify the water, but who's to say her dishwasher raises the temperature to a minimum boiling point of 212 degrees Fahrenheit? It takes at least that to kill impurities in the water like viruses and bacteria."

"Interesting." He didn't even try to hide his grin anymore. "You're really cute when you're passionate about something."

I rolled my eyes. "So, any luck on finding Ruby's body?"

"I talked to the cleaning crew and the bookkeeper, but no one seems to know anything. Creed's Crew was cleaning the Clearview Motel that day, and Tammy Halloway had the day off. Everyone else was out to lunch, but anyone with a key could have slipped in while they were gone, especially knowing the entire staff takes their lunch at the same time."

"It's kind of hard to hide a body, for crying out loud." I rubbed my throbbing temples. "I wouldn't think it would be this difficult to find her. I mean, I didn't really know her, but I feel responsible for her as her next of kin." I set my fork down and pushed my plate away, my appetite all but soured. "And then there's Ma. She'd never survive in jail, and Pop would never survive without her."

"Don't worry. We'll find Ruby. I won't stop looking for her until we do." Nik gazed at me with such sincere eyes. "And I *will* clear your mama's name. I can promise you that." He reached out to hold my hand. *What do I have to do to make you realize I'm not going anywhere, and we're meant to be together? We can work if you just give us a chance.*

I squeezed his hand once before letting go. I knew in my heart that we were meant to be together, but my brain had a mind of its own and refused to listen. Fear could be very debilitating for someone like me.

"I know," I responded to his comment, but secretly was responding to his thoughts as well.

He glanced beyond me and waved.

Turning to see where he looked, I noticed our Greek orthodox priest, Father Papadopoulos, walk in with what looked to be a catholic priest and a nun. Father headed in our direction and stopped by our table.

I smiled a little too bright, still nervous after the chaos both our mamas had caused.

Father nodded once and focused on both of us with a bit of a stern expression. "Detective Stevens. Ms. Ballas. I hope you're both well. I haven't seen either of you in church lately. Don't be like your mamas, now. They have a little while left on their time out, but that doesn't mean I don't expect to see the rest of their families in church."

"My mama raised me right, Father," Nik said.

"She should learn to listen to her own advice," Father replied.

"I agree." Nik nodded. "For the record, she feels terrible. Her bad behavior won't happen again."

"I should hope not." Father's faded blue gaze fell on me, a piece of his thinning gray hair flopping over his forehead. "And what about your mama, Kalli?"

"She's saying her penance every day, Father." I folded my hands. "Ma says her crazy behavior is from the curse."

He nodded gravely. "It might just be. You be careful not to get The Evil Eye curse yourself, now."

"I'm taking every precaution," I said. "Cross my heart."

"I'll see you in church this week then?"

"Absolutely," Nik and I both spoke at once.

"Good." Father gestured to the couple beside him. "This is Father Michael Conery and Sister Mary Margaret."

Father Conery looked to be in his fifties with dark

wavy hair and hazel eyes, while Sister Margaret was younger. Thirties maybe, judging from what I could see of her beneath her habit. A stern, tough face but with warm honey brown eyes. She reminded me of the nuns in the Greek Orthodox school I went to.

Tough but kind.

Nik and I both said hello.

"They're here to help the catholic diocese while Father Comstock is out having surgery," Father Papadopoulos continued. "I trust you'll make them feel welcome during their stay in Clearview."

"Of course," Nik said. "I work for the police department, but you'll see me around town most days."

"I work in Full Disclosure downtown," I chimed in. "If either of you need anything at all, just stop in and my friend Jaz and I will help you out with whatever you need."

"Thank you, Ms. Ballas. That's very kind of you. I just might take you up on that offer." Father Conery smiled at me with the kindest eyes. The Catholic community here in town was going to love him.

Sister Margaret nodded once, sharply. "Much obliged." She scanned the restaurant. "Restrooms?"

I pointed to the back meeting room that many organizations and clubs frequented. "Just down that hall and to the left."

The sister marched off with a no-nonsense pace.

Okay, well *she* might take a little getting used to, but I was a good judge of character. She might be a little intense, but she was a good egg. My eyes caught a movement to the right, and I noticed someone else at a table near the back.

Thalia and Jasper.

I didn't blame her for wanting him to herself away from both our big families. Wise decision with Eleni working at Aphrodite's tonight. Eleni and Thalia had become close since Thalia moved to town, but Eleni and her boyfriend recently broke up and Thalia had been single for a while. They both had their sights set on Jasper and weren't afraid to fight for him. Winning the auction date had finally given her first dibs on the hunky newcomer.

Thalia caught my eye and gave me a thumb's up.

I smiled and gave her a thumb's up back.

Father Conery looked that way pensively for a moment, then said to me, "We should let you and your date get back to your dinner. It was a pleasure to meet you both."

"He's right, of course. Say hello to your families." Father Papadopoulos led the way back to their table, with Sister Mary Margaret joining them moments later.

"I think we need to find a new place for our dates. This one is getting a bit too popular." Nik paid our bill and put his wallet back in his suit coat pocket.

"Agreed."

Now that a lot of Nik's family had moved to Clearview, as well as too many members of mine, trying to find a private moment together was becoming impossible. We were constantly running into someone we knew. Not to mention the Senior Singles Club where Nik's Ma and the Captain had met was held in the back room of Rosalita's once a week. I was beginning to think we would have to go to another town to get a quiet moment alone.

I picked up my utensils and folded them in my napkin, then placed them in my purse. Suddenly, I felt eyes on me again. I glanced around but didn't see anyone looking at me. We stood and made our way to the door, and I bumped into a man.

"Sorry, my fault." The man's gaze met mine, held briefly, then he walked out the door. He was a big guy with a dark buzz cut and dark eyes.

"Who was that?" Nik asked with a frown.

"I don't know. I've seen him around at the Harvest Festival, but I've never met him personally."

"I don't like the way he looked at you."

I chuckled. "You don't like the way any man looks at me."

"Says the woman who bid five thousand dollars for a date with me."

"Touché." I watched the man disappear down the street, alarm bells going off in my head. "Honestly, for once, I have to agree with you. There's something about him that's off." And I'm going to find out why.

"WHAT ARE WE DOING HERE?" Jaz yawned early the next morning as we sat in the parking lot of the Clearview Motel.

I shut off the engine to my Prius. "Following a hunch. I want to know who that big guy I told you about from Rosalita's last night is. He gave me creepy vibes, and it's not the first time I've caught him staring at me. The campgrounds are closed, so this is the only place in town for outsiders to stay."

"And it couldn't wait until after work?"

"Early bird catches the worm, and all that."

"If you say so." Jaz tightened her sweater coat around her to ward off the morning fall chill. "Here's a thought. Maybe he lives in another town within driving distance and is just here for the festival. Not everyone stays over."

"That's true. I just want to rule out all possibilities.

Nik doesn't want me anywhere near him, but he can't check him out without a name. Last I checked there was no crime in being neighborly."

"So that's what the Mosaiko is for."

"No one can resist Ma's Greek chocolate and biscuits."

We walked inside the two-story motel to the small lobby. It used to be a mess and was in dire need of re-modeling, but since Gary Bolin became the manager, the owner Larry Miller had started remodeling. I'd heard he hired Jasper Kent to paint the peeling walls and install new carpet. It was a start. There were still faded lumpy chairs in the lounge beneath a TV that had to be from the eighties, but Larry promised new furniture was next on his list.

The town of Clearview was small and didn't have many other options: a quaint bed and breakfast place on the lake, some cabins in the campground, and Larry Miller's motel. But after several complaints, Larry was finally listening. The man was in his sixties, with thinning combed-over hair and small round spectacles perched on the end of his bulbous nose. He loved attention and reminiscing about the old days, but once he got started, it was nearly impossible to get him to stop.

I glanced around, but Larry wasn't there, thank goodness. Gary Bolin stood at the front desk, talking to Elouise Sinclaire. She smiled at him and slid a large bill in his direction. He nodded once and pocketed the money as she walked out the door with her nose in the air, not sparing Jaz or me a single glance.

Guess we weren't worthy.

These socialites were all about supporting chari-ties, yet they didn't have a charitable bone in their bodies. It was all for show. Fay Baker was exactly the same way. Gary, on the other hand, was a sweetheart.

Gary was in his forties, with dirty blond hair and emerald-green eyes. He used to be a drunk, but he'd cleaned up his act. He briefly had a thing for me until he met and fell for Lisa Chamberlain, a pretty brunette around his age. She worked as a bookkeeper for Maria Danza in her bakery, Sinfully Delicious.

"Hi, Gary, how are you?" I asked as I approached the desk.

Gary looked up and smiled wide when he saw us. "I'm great. I proposed to Lisa, and she said yes."

"That's wonderful," Jaz said. "I'm so happy for you both."

"Perfect timing. Here's a little something for you two to celebrate." I handed him the Mosaiko.

He placed a hand over his heart and closed his eyes. "My favorite." He opened his eyes and winked. "Please tell you mother thank you."

I laughed. "How'd you know I didn't make it?"

"I think the whole town knows your Ma is the cook in the family." Jaz chuckled.

"Well, whoever made it, I appreciate it." Gary smiled.

"So, the parking lot looked packed," I said. "You must be booked full with the festival going on."

"We are. I'm sorry about your moth..." he looked around as if at a loss before continuing, "your Ruby getting murdered, and your ma being a suspect. That's terrible, and now the woman's body is missing? It must be a full moon or something."

"Or a curse," Jaz muttered.

The front door to the hotel chimed, and in walked Winnie Wallaby. She set down a package and read the label. "This package is for Grayson Millbrook. Will you see that he gets it, mate? It's a mite chockers," she said to Gary.

"Thanks, Winnie. I sure will." Gary waved as she left, and he put the package behind the counter.

"Chockers?" I asked.

"Very full," he replied with a grin. "I'm picking up some Australian slang with Winnie around."

I tried not to show my reaction. "So, Grayson Millbrook. Why does that name sound so familiar. Do I know him?"

I knew exactly who he was. Nik said he used to be a regular at Pearl's Place when Ruby danced there, and he asked her out numerous times, but she always said no. I'd looked him up, of course. He was a wealthy businessman. If Ruby was that desperate, why did she say no to him?

Gary rubbed his chin. "Probably not. He's from Cloudsville. He's in town for the festival."

"Oh, so he just got here?"

"No, he got here the day after Ruby died. I only had a vacancy because some people left after the murder. Said he was away on business but didn't want to miss the whole festival. I'm guessing he's still conducting business. That's why he's receiving packages."

"It's not like our Harvest Festival is that special," Jaz said. "And Cloudsville is only one town away. It just seems strange to stay that long in a hotel and work here."

"Like I said, full moon. People are acting really strange these days." Gary shuffled some papers. "Why the mayor scheduled the festival during a full moon is beyond me."

"Speaking of strange people," I said. "Did a large man with a dark buzz cut check in? He had a chain link tattoo around his neck. You can't miss him."

"Yes, actually. Danny Ferrari. Quiet fellow. He checked in before the festival even started. He's not around much, though."

"Thanks, Gary. We won't keep you from your work any longer. I'll tell Ma you said thanks for the Mosaiko. Say hi to Lisa for us."

"Will do." He put the dessert behind the counter. "Say hi to the detectives from us. We'll have to get together sometime soon."

"Sounds good." Jaz led the way outside.

We were almost to my car when I spotted a couple across the parking lot, talking with their heads bent together. I stared with my mouth agape.

"Who's that?" Jaz asked.

"Grayson Millbrook, looking awfully chummy with Newcomer Funeral Home's bookkeeper, Tammy Halloway." Jaz and I shared everything. I had told her all about Grayson and showed her a picture from my research on him.

"How on earth does he know Tammy?" Jaz squinted to see better.

Grayson got into his car and drove away.

"I don't know, but we're about to find out." I headed over toward Tammy's car and reached her just before she pulled away.

She rolled down the window, and her cheeks flushed pink. "Ms. Ballas and Ms. Alvarez, I'm surprised to see you here."

"I could say the same, Ms. Halloway." I narrowed my eyes at her. "How do you know Grayson Millbrook?"

She thrust her chin up. "That's none of your business."

"He used to frequent the strip club where Ruby used to work and wasn't pleased when she kept turning him down for a date. Now she's not only dead but missing. As her next of kin, I would say that's my business."

"Look, I'm just trying to honor his privacy. He was in love with Ruby, so when he found out she was murdered, he came to Clearview the very next day to pay his respects. He came to the funeral home while I was working. I let him say his goodbyes to her before she went missing."

I blinked, processing what I'd just heard. "Did you give him your key?"

Her mouth opened wide. "What? Good lord, no."

"Then what exactly *did* you give him?" Jaz looked at the motel sign and then at Tammy with a raised brow.

Tammy gasped. "Friendship, that's all. If we're done here, I have things to do. Today is my day off."

"By all means. No one is keeping you here against your will. You were always free to go." I stepped back, and she drove off at a much quicker pace than I'd ever seen her. She was hiding something.

We weren't done. Not by a long shot.

CHAPTER 8

J az and I stopped into Sinfully Delicious on our way into work at Full Disclosure. I'd promised her I would feed her sweet tooth and buy her a very large cup of coffee for being my wing woman.

We walked inside and Jaz immediately placed her order to the young girl working the counter. Maria came out of her office in the back, poked her head into her bookkeeper Lisa's office and said something, then came up front carrying a package.

"Hi, Maria, how are you and Sully?" Jaz asked.

Maria and Jaz used to be enemies because Jaz stole the local carpenter Johnny Hogan away from her. In Jaz's defense, she didn't know Maria and Johnny were a thing. But it all worked out for the best when Maria took Sully Anderson, the UPS driver, away from Jaz. Now that Jaz was with Boomer, everyone was happy and friends again.

"We're great!" Maria brushed her long black hair over her shoulder and thrust out her left hand, wiggling her fingers, showing off a diamond ring. "He proposed last night. Isn't it so romantic?" Her cherubic cheeks glowed.

My eyes sprang wide. First Lisa and Gary. Now Maria and Sully. There must be something in those baked goods. I stepped away from the counter.

"That's wonderful," Jaz said. "You look fabulous, by the way."

Maria beamed. "Just for that, I'm adding one of my signature cinnamon rolls to your order on me."

Jaz squealed and clapped her hands.

Maria laughed. "Anything else for you, Kalli?"

"Oh, no, I'm never hungry in the morning. Just my organic tea, please, but thank you for asking." No way was I touching the wedding pastries. Besides, I kept a stash of healthy organic options in my loft. I cringed thinking of what all that sugar and white flour was doing to Jaz's insides, but that was a comment I would keep to myself, same as I did with Ma's desserts.

Sully came in, his curly caramel hair and olive complexion complimenting his brown and tan delivery uniform. He waved to us, kissed Maria's cheek, took the package from her and then stopped by a table before leaving.

I did a double take.

Grayson Millbrook sat at a table in the far corner. I hadn't noticed him when we came in. He and Sully had a conversation, and then Sully nodded once and left. Grayson made eye contact with me, held my gaze for a moment, and then looked away as he took a phone call.

"You ready?" Jaz gave me a funny look. "Are you okay?"

"I will be once we're outside."

After we cleared the door and crossed the street, I didn't speak until we entered Full Disclosure.

"What's going on?" Jaz asked.

"Did you see who was inside the bakery?"

She frowned. "No, why?"

"Grayson Millbrook."

"Well, we know he's in town. Why is his being here surprising?"

"It's not surprising, but his reaction to me is. When he saw me, he stared at me like he knew me. I've researched him, but I've never met him in person before."

"He might not know you, but you look exactly like Ruby. If what Tammy says is true and he was in love with Ruby, then looking at you has to be like looking at a ghost."

"I guess you're right, but his look was so intense. It was rather unnerving. And Sully stopped to talk to him on the way out. Why?"

"Well, Gary did say Grayson was staying in town conducting business, and Sully is a delivery driver. Maybe it has something to do with that."

"Maybe? I'm probably just paranoid. So much has happened since my biological mother randomly showed up in my life after twenty-nine years. At least now I know who I come from, but I almost wish I never did."

∼

"KALLI, WHAT ARE YOU DOING HERE?" Detective Stevens —he was most definitely in detective mode now— asked when I showed up at Tammy Halloway's house. He stood outside in the driveway while Boomer and the CSI crew were inside with Tammy.

"I heard what happened to poor Tammy and wanted to see if she was okay." I'd barely been at work when the rumor mill started buzzing that someone broke into her house and ransacked the place.

"And I heard what happened when you accosted Tammy at the Clearview Motel this morning." He raised one thick dark eyebrow and stared at me with those piercing blue eyes of his.

He knew they were my undoing, and he used them wisely.

I gasped in true Ballas drama fashion. "I did no such thing. I simply brought Gary and Lisa Ma's Mosaiko this morning on my way into work. They *are* my friends, you know. I was just trying to be neighborly."

"Nothing about the Clearview Motel is *on your way* into work, and they're nowhere near our neighborhood. Seems to me you went out of your way to meddle in this case when I specifically told you not to. The captain doesn't want you to."

"And if I remember correctly, he didn't want you to meddle in your mother's case, either. Guess I listen about as well as you did. And if I didn't meddle, I never would have found out that big guy from Rosalita's Place who looked at me funny is staying at the motel, and his name is Danny Ferrari." I gave him a pointed look.

He paused a minute, then relented. "Nice job, Ballas, but I don't want you to do anything else that's even remotely linked to this case. Am I clear?"

"As rain." He just had no clue rain was full of impurities like dust, fine sand, clay, dirt, and biological contaminants just like my response.

"As far as Grayson goes, Tammy told me all about how he loved Ruby. She's helping him to cope with the loss of a loved one."

"She's a bookkeeper, not a funeral director. It's Wally's job to comfort people, not hers. Besides, even you said Ruby wanted nothing to do with Grayson, so I wouldn't exactly call him a loved one."

"How do you know that?" My favorite pair of baby blues narrowed as they nailed me with their icy glare. "I know that I didn't *tell* you that."

Whoops. I fluttered my eye lashes over my innocent green ones. "Well, you weren't exactly whispering when you were talking to Captain Crenshaw at brunch, so I assumed it wasn't a secret."

He snorted. "Nice try. I *knew* you were eavesdropping when Ma caught you outside the sunroom door."

"So, who do you think broke into Tammy's house?" I stepped around him and looked at the front door.

No damage.

Nik let my change in subject slide. "We don't know yet. They came in through the back. Picked the lock by the looks of it. Just like with the funeral home, Tammy didn't have any security cameras."

"And obviously no dead bolts." I could never understand how some people felt so relaxed and comfortable. My place was locked to the max.

"Whoever it was trashed the place but didn't take anything. Either someone has something against Tammy, or they were looking for something specific."

"Interesting. Well, Grayson couldn't have broken in. He was with Tammy at the hotel and then at Sinfully Delicious for breakfast. Jaz and I saw him when we stopped by to grab breakfast before work. Don't you think it's strange he's conducting business here when he lives one town away. Why stay if Ruby is dead?"

Nik rubbed his whiskered jaw. "The festival is still going on. And Ruby's body still hasn't been found." He shrugged. "Who knows. Maybe he needs closure."

"Or maybe he killed her because she turned him

down. You know, the whole if I can't have you, then no one can."

"You're reaching, Ballas. He has an alibi for the night of her murder. He didn't get to town until the next day when he heard she'd been murdered. How could he have murdered her when he wasn't even in town yet?"

"His connections might have done the deed, but I wouldn't be surprised if he ordered the hit. Danny Ferrari sure looks like he could be a hit man."

"You really should stop watching so many movies, Ms. Ballas," said a man's voice from behind us.

We whirled around, and there stood Grayson Millbrook in the flesh.

~

"What is this I hear about *you* causing trouble?" Ma crossed her arms over her apron at Aphrodite's that evening just before the dinner crowd was set to start rolling in.

I was picking up a to-go order to take home, but I had hoped to escape before a lecture from Ma. Dinner for one as Detective Dreamy wasn't too pleased with me at the moment. Grayson was a smooth operator. He'd had all the right answers for Nik and acted like a devastated friend of Tammy's, rushing to her side to be of help.

I wasn't buying any of it, and I'd said as much.

My theory was he came to see if he could find whatever the perpetrator had missed when ransacking Tammy's place. That theory had Grayson threatening a lawsuit and Detective Dreamy threatening to lock me up. So, I'd left.

"I don't know what you're talking about, Ma."

"You know I gave that Mosaiko to you for you and your man. You know, to make up. It wasn't meant for anyone else. No wonder your man so angry."

I crossed my arms over my chest. "I thought he was on your bad list for naming you a suspect in Ruby's murder?"

"Technicalities." She waved her hand. "He's still your man. Good looking and Greek. Enough said."

"He's not my man, Ma. We were dating, then we weren't, and now we are again...I think."

"You wouldn't have to think if you'd kept my Mosaiko." She pointed at me, giving me a knowing look. "Give a man sweets, and he be sweet to you."

"Look, it's been a long day. I just want to go home and go to bed."

"It's been a long day because you cause trouble. Why you give Gary my Mosaiko? He's a good boy. He called to thank me, but it no for him."

"You didn't tell him that, did you?"

"Kalliope Ballas, I have manners."

"I know. I just wanted to do something nice for Gary and Lisa because they're my friends."

"Bah, I know you." She stared at me for a long moment. "You trying to solve this case for your mama."

"I just can't shake this feeling that her murder has something to do with someone from her past. I mean, she was a stripper. There had to be drama surrounding that. Her boss, the other strippers, the clientele...so many possibilities," I said more to myself, thinking out loud.

"Hmmmm." Ma snapped me out of my thoughts, and I watched her look off, concentrating hard. "You might have a point. A striptease can drive a man wild. I no lie. Cousin Gregor went to a strip club and came out cross-eyed. He was never the same again."

"Who no the same?" Aunt Tasoula sashayed in wearing an outfit that was two sizes too small, lipstick that was too dark, and her hair teased like she was starring in an eighties' hair band rock video.

"Cousin Gregor."

"Ohhh, it's true." She shook her head gravely, then cocked her head to the side. "Maybe I should try teasing the strip."

"On who?" Ma perked up.

"Opa! My table's ready." Aunt Tasoula swayed her way into the dining room to join Tate Hemsworth.

"One date my foot," Ma muttered, then snapped her spine straight and marched back into the kitchen.

I picked up my to-go order, wondering if I'd just caused even more trouble. I turned around to leave, then stopped short. "Hi, Jasper." I peeked beyond him. "Where's Thalia?"

He was a handsome man but shy and quiet. He ran a hand through his dark wavy hair, and his green eyes finally met mine. "Thalia's a nice woman, but we already had our auction date. I'm actually here to do some work for your mother."

"Oh, what kind of work?"

"I've been doing a little work for her on the side since I got into town. I met her at the festival the first day. Now I'm hanging more shelves in the pantry. Fixing some sheetrock from water damage." He shrugged. "Small stuff."

"Oh, nice. I'm sure she appreciates it."

He nodded once and started to head to the kitchen but stopped and looked back at me. "You're lucky to have her. Your pop, too."

I blinked. "Thank you. I have been blessed for sure."

I heard a sound to the right and saw Jasper's eyes

look that way and soften. I turned to see who he was looking at.

Eleni.

Eleni looked up and noticed him looking at her. A slow smile spread wide across her heart-shaped face, and she waved at him. I looked back at him, and his face flushed crimson. He nodded once to her and then quickly walked into the kitchen.

Thalia had won the bid, but it was clear she certainly hadn't won the war.

I headed out the door and climbed into my car just in time. A soft rain started to fall. I drove in silence, with no radio on, just listening to the soft patter of raindrops. It had a calming effect on me as I took several deep breaths and willed my body to release the tension from the day.

The next thing I knew I was home.

I glanced to the other half of the driveway, but Nik wasn't home yet. Grabbing my belongings, I darted out of my car and let myself inside my house. Prissy was waiting impatiently for me by her food bowl.

"I know, girl, I'm sorry I'm late."

I fed her and then changed into yoga pants and a soft sweater. All I wanted to do was have a glass of wine and watch a movie. I was just starting to open a bottle when I heard a noise coming from out back. I set the bottle down and went over to the sliding back door to my deck. Peeking outside, I gasped then jumped back.

There was a shadow out there.

My heart raced and it took three tries for me to get up the nerve to look again. I didn't see anything. I flipped on the light and searched again. Nothing. I ran to the front of my house and looked outside. Again, nothing.

And just like that the tension was back.

It was probably my imagination, but Nik wasn't home, and with him frustrated with me, I didn't really want to see him right now. So, I did what any woman would do. I called my best friend.

"Hey, girl, what's up?" Jaz said. And that was all it took.

I burst into tears.

All I heard was, "I'll be there in five minutes," before the line went dead.

CHAPTER 9

There was a knock on my door. My heart sped up and my eyes darted around my living room. I snatched an umbrella hanging from my coat tree, and I peeked out the front window. Blowing out a huge breath, I opened the door.

Jaz stood there, holding Wolfgang by the collar. "Look who I found scratching at your door."

His entire body quivered with the urge to jump on me, but we had come to an agreement of sorts. He knew that if he sat still, I would pet him on the top of his head, far away from the saliva dripping from his mouth. And if he was *very* still, I might just pet him twice, but I drew the line at belly rubs.

I gagged.

"So, you naughty boy, how did you get out?" I reached forward, and his quivering increased, but he didn't jump. I pet the top of his massive St. Bernard head, and his eyes rolled back on a whine.

"I swear you're the only one who can control him. I don't know how you do it. The minute you're not around, his good behavior goes right out the window." Jaz scoffed as she tightened her grip on his collar with one hand and brushed the leaves from the tree in my front yard off her leggings with the other.

"Oh, no. What happened?"

"He literally tackled me to the ground the second I stepped out of my car, and he nearly took my arm off by dragging me to your door. My girls are so much better behaved than this beast."

"He's just a little misunderstood. I can relate," I said calmly. "You can let go of him now. I've got him."

Her eyes widened. "Are you sure?"

I nodded.

"Wow, you two have come a long way." She released Wolf.

Wolfgang's muscles twitched, but he didn't move an inch. He just kept his eyes locked on mine, waiting for my command.

"You can go on in and help yourself to some wine. I'll be there in a minute." I looked down at Wolf. "Come on, boy. Let's get you home."

I headed over to Nik's with Wolfgang right beside me and grabbed the key Nik kept hidden in a lockbox beneath the bushes. He'd given me the combination in case I ever needed to get in. I didn't have a lockbox for my half of the house. The thought of someone having access to my place when I wasn't there kind of freaked me out.

But Nik wasn't just anyone.

I frowned, not ready to think about that right now. I brought Wolfgang inside Nik's half of the house and stopped short. His back sliding door was open. I closed the door and locked it, then looked out at his yard but didn't see anyone there. There was, however, a hole between our fences and my gate was open.

Did Wolf see someone in my yard, escape through the slider Nik kept cracked for him to get fresh air, and then break through our fences to protect me? Wolf definitely made the hole, but there was no way he could open a latched gate. I shivered and crossed my arms, stepping away from the sliding door.

Wolf whined and cocked his head when I looked at him.

My heart melted. "I'm okay, boy." This time I pet him with both hands and shocked myself by kissing the top of his head.

He licked his lips.

I straightened and pointed my finger at him. "Easy, pal. This does *not* mean you can kiss me back."

I gave him one of his dog bones, then I scrubbed my hands in the sink and wiped my mouth before heading out the door. I secured the lock and hid the key once more then walked back over to my place. After closing the gate to my fence, I walked out front and was just about to open my door when I felt the sensation of being watched again. There! A shadow ducking behind the trees. A rustle of leaves. The hairs on my neck standing at attention.

This time I wasn't imagining it.

I blinked and then squinted harder to see. Nothing. I quickly slipped inside and locked my door then took several steps back. Turning around, I saw Jaz sitting at the kitchen table, watching me with concern.

"You're really jumpy. And you cried earlier, which breaks my heart every time. Is everything okay?"

"I feel like I'm losing my mind." I joined her at the table and smiled over the glass of wine she had waiting for me.

"I would too if I had gone through everything you have."

"Ever since Ruby died, I feel like I'm being watched. At work, in town, and now at home. I swear I saw a shadow earlier. And when I brought Wolf home, I noticed the latch was undone to my half of the yard, and Wolfgang put a hole through the fence. I'm sure he was trying to protect me and scared the person off. But even now when I just came back inside, I felt eyes on me."

"But you barely knew Ruby. Why would someone be after you?"

"I have no idea. Maybe because I'm listed as her next of kin, they think I know more than I do? I know Ruby needed money. I just don't know what exactly she was involved in. Maybe I'm cursed like Ma."

"You don't seriously believe in The Evil Eye curse, do you?" Jaz arched a brow high and took another sip of her wine.

I shrugged, not sure what I believed anymore.

My phone rang. "Speaking of Ma. It's Pop, and that's never good." I answered and put him on speaker phone. "Pop, what's wrong?"

"It's your mama."

I frowned at Jaz. "What about Ma? I just saw her a couple hours ago when I picked up my to-go order right before the dinner rush. She seemed fine."

"It's the curse. I just know it. Your mama got the tummy ache from out of nowhere. I never see her wail and moan like that. I think she's possessed. You're Uncle Aeries was possessed once. I try to get your mama to wrap her tummy in aloe and Duct tape, but she no listen. She make your Aunt Tasoula end her date with that Viking and take her home. Straight away."

Jaz arched a brow, obviously not buying Ma's *sickness* any more than I was.

"If Aunt Tasoula is with her, then why are you calling me?"

"Because they no answer their mobile devices. They no answer the email on the line, either. What if this curse has made something horrible happen?"

I set my untouched wine down and sighed. "What do you want me to do, Pop?"

"I can't leave the restaurant. We're packed. Can you go check on your mama? It would make your pop so happy."

"Sure thing."

"Oh, and Kalliope?"

"Yes?"

"Wear the hashtag suit."

"The what?"

"You know, the thingy that makes you look like Buzz Lightyear."

"You mean a hazmat suit?"

"Ya ya. That's a what I say. Or your papou has a beebeeper suit. He beeps, and they fly away. Just don't look in your mama's eyes. She's like a Medusa. I no want you to get The Evil Eye curse, too. I gotta go." He groaned before shouting, "Frona, no put clean dishes in the washer and dirty ones on the bar. Go see Yia-Yia." He grunted. "This day no good." And then he hung up.

"Well, are we hitting the road?" Jaz finished the rest of her wine and set her empty glass next to my full one. "You're driving."

"Are you sure you can come with me? Where's Boomer?"

"Out with Nik. Apparently, he had a bad day as well."

"Then I'm definitely ready to go." I covered my wineglass with a napkin. "We'll check on Ma, I'll drop you off, then I'm headed straight to bed. I can't afford for anything else to happen in one day."

~

"JUST AS I SUSPECTED," I said.

We'd stopped by Ma's house and then Aunt Tasoula's house as well as her salon. They were nowhere to be found, but I had a strong idea of where they might be, and it wasn't good. If I was right, we were all going to be in trouble.

"Where do you think they went?" Jaz asked.

"Well, when I picked up my dinner, Ma talked about how she knew I was only trying to help clear her name, but she didn't want me to get into any more trouble. I mentioned I wasn't getting anywhere by looking into leads here in town, and I wondered if maybe the murder had to do with something or someone from Ruby's past." I paused a beat and looked Jaz in the eye. "Then we got on the subject of strippers."

"No way! You don't think Ophelia and Tasoula would go to Pearl's Place, do you?" Jaz gaped at me with a mixture of horrified and amused speculation.

"Oh, I wouldn't put anything past those two lately." I turned on the road headed out of town.

Jaz sucked in a sharp breath. "Oh, my Lord, are we actually going to a strip club?" Her eyes grew wide with a look I knew all too well.

"What choice do we have?" I cringed, thinking I might never be the same again by the time the night was over.

"Fine by me." She squealed and clapped her hands. "I have always wanted to go to a strip club. It's on my bucket list."

I puckered my face. "Not me. Do you know how many germs are in that place? I can't even think about it, or I'll break out in hives."

"Then don't think, just drive, sister. The night's not getting any younger, and neither are we."

"Just don't get any crazy ideas. We're there to find Ma and Aunt Tasoula, and then go home. That's it."

"Whatever you say." She stared out the window all innocent like.

She wasn't fooling anyone.

A little while later, we arrived at the club. We climbed out of my Prius and headed inside. Scanning the dancefloor, we saw a sea of men and women dancing. I was in yoga pants, a sweater, and sneakers. Meanwhile, Jaz wore trendy leggings, an off the shoulder blouse, and heels. She looked way more appropriate for a night on the town.

Pushing our way through the crowd, we searched for Ma and Aunt Tasoula with no luck. Maybe they hadn't actually gone to Pearl's Place. Loud music boomed through the speakers. Jaz started dancing, and I was about to tell her we should leave before we both get in trouble, but then Pearl herself—I'd looked her up—grabbed the microphone.

"Who says blondes have more fun? And age is just a number, my friends. These feisty gals are a little new to stripping, but let's give them a warm welcome and see if they have what it takes to be one of Pearl's gems."

"No way," Jaz muttered.

"Oh, no," I groaned.

Aunt Tasoula's hands moved at the speed of Grease lightning as she sang Born to Jive the Hand at the top of her lungs with a few opa's thrown in. Her outfit rivaled Sandy's during the movie finale.

"She's definitely been into the Ouzo," Jaz said.

"Ya think?" I cringed.

Meanwhile, Ma was definitely channeling Rizzo's outfit with a major frizzo haloing her beehive

"Oh. My. God." Jaz's jaw fell wide open. "What is your mother doing?"

Ma gave up on the Hand Jive and started jerking her body about in short, choppy moves as though she were Wall-E the robot. Apparently not what the crowd had in mind, judging by the sounds of their booing and yelling at her to get off the stage. Ma huffed, and then her face transformed into a look I knew all too well.

The Determinator.

Holding her arm at the elbow, she sliced the air like a meat cutter short circuiting into overdrive as she pivoted back and forth, and back and forth. For Zeus's sake, she looked like my cousin Yanni's turbo sprinkler, twisting about as she watered the stage.

"Please, gods of Mount Olympus, have mercy on me and make them stop," I whispered, rubbing my temples.

"Honey, I already tried that. It didn't work," a woman said from beside me. "My eyes will never be the same."

"Work the crowd, ladies, or get off the stage," Pearl said into the microphone with a tone that meant business.

"They're working the crowd, all right." Jaz glanced around with concerned eyes. "Working them into an angry frenzy."

The boos and catcalls grew louder and more negative.

I felt like I was watching a really bad reality show. I knew it was awful, but I couldn't look away.

A sheen of sweat glazed Ma's forehead as the colorful lights reflected off her face. I could tell she was getting frustrated and exhausted. I was worried about her heart palpitations, but she wasn't about to be out-done by Aunt Tasoula. Since her last move hadn't pro-duced any better results, she held her arms shoulder-width apart out in front of her as she bounced and piv-oted slightly to the left and right.

Someone in the crowd yelled, "You've got to be kidding me. Not the Shopping Cart. Where'd you learn to dance? A grocery store?"

Ma gave the man a gesture I couldn't unsee and quickly transitioned into yet another dance. What on earth was this one supposed to be—the Lawn Mower? Her bat wings were working overtime as she kept pulling that imaginary rope hard.

"Pull harder," another guy in the crowd yelled.

Ma immediately let go of her imaginary rope and turned sideways as she moved into another dance, let-ting loose a string of words the man was lucky he couldn't hear. She pushed off the toe of one foot while sliding the other backward across the stage, then switched legs and repeated. She even added her own twist of flapping her arms at her sides.

"Don't improvise, woman. You ain't no swan. Ya look like a goose about to take off, and it ain't pretty!" someone else yelled.

She quickly dropped her arms and faced the loud, rumbling crowd, looking like she was gonna unleash a can of whoopdido, as she liked to say.

Aunt Tasoula jumped on the pole center-stage and twirled around and around, sliding down an inch with every spin as she sang, "Ring around the poley!" She somehow ended up topsy turvy, with her legs wrapped around the pole above her head and her hands breaking her fall as she firmly flopped on the wooden floor. She quickly rolled to her side, posed, and blew a kiss to the crowd.

I cringed, hoping her hand didn't touch her lips after grabbing that pole.

Ma scowled at her and marched to the front of the stage. For a minute, I thought she might jump into the crowd and unleash her inner Hades. Instead, she thrust her hands out in front of her and clenched them into fists. Bringing them into her chest and then away, she started a pumping motion. She lifted her knees up and down and slid her feet back and forth as though she were marching in place.

"What in all of Mount Olympus is that supposed to be?" Jaz asked.

"That, my friend, would be Ma's version of the Running Man. I do believe it's time to start drinking."

The crowd cheered wildly, and I looked at the stage to see what had them so excited. I bit my lip and winced, finding it hard to watch. A woman as endowed as my mother had no business doing the Running *anything!*

Ma paused, her face registering her shock at finally winning the crowd over, then her mouth twisted into a smug smile as she looked at Aunt Tasoula. Lord have mercy, she started running even faster, her bouncing assets keeping pace with the rhythm of her feet.

Her bunions were going to be killing her tomorrow.

Aunt Tasoula jumped up, and the race was on.

Little did they know they weren't the ones the crowd had gone wild over. A group of strippers had slipped on stage behind them and looked as though they were trying to help get the crowd riled up. The dirtier they danced, the crazier the crowd became, and...oh good grief...the faster the Pink Ladies ran.

The crowd started chanting, "Strip! Strip! Strip!"

Pearl said firmly, "Enough with the tease, ladies, it's time to strip. This isn't a danceathon."

Ma and Aunt Tasoula both stopped moving, as horrified expressions crossed their faces. They finally spotted Jaz and me, staring them down with crossed arms and tapping toes. They headed for the edge of the stage.

"Not so fast, ladies. When I caught you in the dressing room in the back, you said you were strippers. I have yet to see you take anything off. You're not getting off that stage until I do."

"We have to do something," I said.

"Follow my lead," Jaz replied.

She led the way onto the stage. I quickly followed, holding my breath every step of the way, hoping the germs being unleashed by the strippers weren't airborne.

"Now we're talking," someone shouted.

"House rules, ladies. You step on my stage, you strip," Pearl purred.

I froze.

Jaz faced me and grabbed my hands, looking me in the eyes. *I've got you, just follow my lead. We have to take something off, but she didn't say what we had to take off.*

I nodded my agreement. For once I was so happy about my mind-reading ability and Jaz being the only one who knew about it.

Ma and Aunt Tasoula looked at us, then at each other and did what we did.

Jaz let go of my hands and pulled the hair band from her hair as she swayed back and forth. I did the same, and so did the Pink Ladies. I could see the wheels spinning in Jaz's mind for another safe item to remove.

I kicked my shoes off, and they followed suit. Now what? We were running out of things to *safely* take off. Ma and Aunt Tasoula caught on and winked at us, then twirled around us as they wrapped one of their extra scarves around both of us, then let go. We resumed our positions and all of us slid our scarves off. I looked stiff, Jaz looked sexy, and the Pink Ladies looked like flag twirlers in a marching band.

We all took a bow and made a beeline for stage left.

"Take off something real, ladies. Show more skin, and I won't consider the night a waste." Pearl narrowed her eyes at us, her bouncers standing on either side of her, looking more than ready to get their hands on us.

We all stood there and stared at each other.

Aunt Tasoula shrugged, not looking too upset at the idea. "I be the hero. You no worry. It's only flesh."

She moved closer to the edge of the stage and slowly grabbed the edge of her shirt, when suddenly the fire alarm went off. Everyone started running for the door, given a recent dance club fire that killed several people. Not wasting a single moment, we grabbed our belongings and scrambled off the stage, heading outside to our cars.

"Whatever you found had better be worth it, Ma," I said as I slipped my sneakers back on.

"Yeah, what in the world were you two thinking coming to a place like this," Jaz added from beside me, slipping her feet back in her heels.

"I could say the same thing," said a male voice from behind me.

"And I won't say what I'm thinking," said another male voice from behind Jaz.

We looked at each other and held hands, as Jaz's thoughts rang out loud and clear. *Your Ma was right. Nothing good comes from teasing the strip.*

CHAPTER 10

"What in the world were you two thinking?" Nik asked us as we sat around my kitchen table. Jaz's car was still here so Boomer would drive her home in that since Nik had picked him up in his car to go out. They'd waited in the car until Tate Hemsworth had picked up Aunt Tasoula and Ma.

"We were thinking Ma and Aunt Tasoula were causing trouble again," I said. "Ma faked being sick and dragged Aunt Tasoula with her as her accomplice."

"How did she know about Pearl's Place?" Nik asked.

"That was my fault. I was sharing my theory that maybe Ruby's killer was someone from her past, and Ma knows she was a stripper from Cloudsville. She got impatient waiting around for other people to clear her name, so she went snooping in the dressing rooms there. When they got caught, they said they were strippers, so Pearl put them to the test."

"So, you dragged Jaz along as *your* accomplice to

save the day," Boomer said without the hint of even a smirk.

"Something like that," I admitted sheepishly, feeling my cheeks heat, then I picked up the glass of wine I'd left on my counter—covered of course—and finally was able to take a much-needed big sip.

"Oh, please, you're not getting in trouble alone, Kalli. I was more than happy to go help a friend in need." Jaz put her hands on her hips, eying her boyfriend. "How did you guys know where we were anyway?"

"You're my girlfriend. We share locations on our phones, remember?" He put his hands on his own hips.

"When Amos didn't hear back from Kalli after she checked on Ophelia and Tasoula, he called me." Nik's eyes locked on mine. "I had no idea where you were because *we* don't share anything." He took a big swig of his beer.

I looked away and took another sip of my wine. "We sort of share a fridge since I keep your favorite beer in there." I smiled until my teeth showed.

His mouth remained in a firm line. "And I keep wine in my fridge for you. That's not what I meant, and you know it."

"On that note, I'm going to take my girl home." Boomer stood and held out his hand to Jaz. "The pups need to go out."

Jaz mouthed *Sorry* to me and followed Boomer outside to the car.

"Maybe I should leave, too." Nik started to get up.

"No, stay," I quickly said. "Please."

He sat back in his chair and waited for me to speak.

"I don't like this tension between us."

"I don't either, but every time I think we're making progress, you take a step back." He rubbed his whiskered jaw, the lines around his eyes looking deeper." I felt bad because he looked exhausted. I was sure the pressure of clearing Ma's name on top of worrying about us was getting to him.

"I'm sorry. I don't mean to take any steps back. There's just so much going on right now. I can't take any more added stress."

His face softened. "I know. Just when we were starting to move forward, your world got turned upside down. I'm not trying to make things even harder for you, I promise. As long as I know you still want to be in this…whatever we're calling it…with me, then I'll be as patient as you need me to be."

"I'm not going anywhere, Detective." I smiled a little shyly and folded my yoga pants clad legs beneath me. "I like this…whatever we're calling it."

"Good."

We sat there just looking at each other, and it felt nice. It felt right.

"So," I cleared my throat, "do you have any updates on the case? I know you don't want me involved, but I need to know what's going on for my own sanity. I'm getting really worried that Ma is going to take the fall for Ruby's murder. She has no alibi, she knew how to tamper with the latch, she has motive, and she had means with her plans to meet Ruby there to bribe her to leave town for good."

"I put a tail on Danny Ferrari. He's been spotted in Vincenzo Ricci's restaurant after hours with Vincenzo himself. It could be nothing, but Vinny has been looking for a way to get back at your mama. And, frankly, I didn't like the way Danny looked at you when we left Rosalita's. I wouldn't put it past Vinny to be cooking something up devious with Danny. What about You? Did you find out anything at Pearl's Place?"

"Well, it turns out Ruby was a drug addict as well." This was one time I really did wish I had Ma's genes.

"How do you know this for sure?"

"When you and Boomer were sitting in the car waiting for us, Ma started talking. Ma and Aunt Tasoula got the scoop from the other strippers before we got to the club. If people think you're a fellow stripper, they apparently don't hold anything back. Ma only agreed to ride home with Tate Hemsworth and Aunt Tasoula because she knew it was the lesser of two evils than explaining that she teased the strip to Pop."

"I'm sure he found out as soon as she got home"

"At least she had the ride home to figure out what to say."

"I can't imagine that conversation." Nik winced.

"You and me both." I played with the edges of my napkin before adding, "But there's more to the story."

"I'm listening."

I couldn't quite meet Nik's eyes. "Ruby's fellow strippers told Ma my biological father was a drug dealer." I sighed and finally looked at him, feeling like a loser myself. I knew I wasn't. I couldn't control who I came from, but a part of me worried if any of these traits were hereditary. If I would become what they were.

If Nik would still want me.

His eyes were filled with sympathy and compassion, not judgement, easing my mind. "I know what you're thinking, Kalli, but you're not your father. And you're definitely not your mother."

"Thank you for that." I took a deep breath before continuing. "That's how Ruby met him, I guess. She only told me that he had quirks like I do, so they were only together one time. He didn't have my gift, so I'm sure it was difficult for him."

"Your gift?" Nik gave me a funny look.

I felt the color drain from my face. "My gift of a personality," I teased, my throat suddenly dry. I pushed the last of my wine away.

Nik's lips tipped up in amused puzzlement.

"Anyway, he split after he got her pregnant, and she found a new dealer. Only, according to the strippers Ma and Aunt Tasoula talked to, Ruby was afraid of this new dealer. She got in over her head, into much heavier stuff apparently, and owed the dealer a lot of money. When she didn't have it, she took off without settling up. She didn't settle up with Pearl, either, and that woman is pretty scary herself."

"Interesting. I wondered what you ladies were all talking about when Boomer and I waited in the car."

"Yeah, my backstory's a real winner, isn't it?"

"Maybe not, but *you* are. You got lucky with the Ballas clan. Imagine what your life would have been like if Amos and Ophelia hadn't adopted you."

"My worst nightmare." I used to think my family was crazy. Now I realized they were normal sane people, just loud and over-the-top sometimes. My biological parents were the crazy ones. I needed to make sure my adoptive parents knew just how much I loved and appreciated them. I realized I didn't say that nearly enough.

"Okay, so let's think this through." Nik ran a hand through his messy dark hair then looked at me. "The dealer could have come after Ruby to Clearview, stalked her, and then struck when she was alone in the park before your ma got there."

"That's true." My jaw fell open as realization

struck. "The dealer could be the person who's going around ransacking places of anyone who had anything to do with Ruby. They could be looking for their money."

"You have a point. Ruby's room at the motel was torn apart but nothing taken. Same with Tammy's house. Tammy had access to Ruby." He looked at me with concern. "So did you. You need to be alert because whoever is doing these things could come after you next."

I felt my stomach bottom out. "I think they already did."

"What? When."

"I keep feeling like someone is watching me. Around town, at work, and even at home. I know I saw someone outside in my back yard tonight."

He sat forward. "Why didn't you call me immediately."

I shrugged. "At first, I thought maybe I imagined it. By the way, Wolfgang got out earlier. I brought him home. Your slider was wide open, and he broke through the fence into my half of the backyard."

"I always leave it open a crack for him, but he never usually touches it. Something must have drawn his attention for him to push through it. But to break through the fence as well? He wouldn't do that unless he didn't like what he was sensing. We both know how protective he is of you."

"That's why I think I *wasn't* imagining it. I'm sure Wolf heard someone back there, too, and was trying to protect me. The person must have run out my gate because they left it open, and Wolf ended up on my front steps."

Nik frowned. "I'll fix the fence tomorrow. I don't

think it's a good idea for you to be home alone. Not after this."

"I would normally agree with you, but you're only one wall away if I need you. I promise I will call this time."

"Okay," he said reluctantly. "But for the record, I don't like this."

"Duly noted." For the record...I didn't like it, either. I was through with letting people I barely knew or didn't know at all affect me. One way or another, I would find out who was messing with me.

And then they would see who could be the craziest one of all.

THE NEXT DAY I arranged the latest collection of my Kalli Originals designs on a rack in Full Disclosure. The fall collection was really taking off. The doorbell chimed and in walked one of Jaz's regulars, Lois Flannigan, who was always first in line for a sale.

Her husband, Michael Flannigan, owned Flannigan's Pub. He worked a lot of hours, and they didn't have children, so he gave Lois carte blanche on the credit cards to keep her happy. If you wanted to know the best deal in town on anything or the latest gossip, then Lois was the woman you talked to.

Elouise Sinclaire was with Lois, who was running around treating her like royalty, explaining where the best finds were. Elouise caught Jaz and me looking at her, and she smiled then held out her hand. "I don't think we've met. I'm Elouise Sinclaire."

Jaz shook her hand. "I'm Jazlyn Alvarez, owner of Full Disclosure. It's very nice to meet you. I hope you find something you like today."

"Oh, Mrs. Flannigan has been quite informative." She smoothed back her short, burgundy hair, her gray eyes sparkling. "I'm sure I'll find something to my liking."

"Please, call me Lois." As a redhead with fair skin, her rosy apple cheeks blossomed even more.

"Well, thank you, darling." Elouise patted Lois's hand and then held her palm out, eyeing me curiously. "And you are...?"

"Kalli Ballas. I design the lingerie you see here." I shook her hand and held on for a minute.

Elouise studied me closer. *What an interesting woman you are. I bet you know everything about the people in this town.* I pulled my hand away discreetly and shoved it in my suit coat pocket. When she looked away, I applied hand sanitizer.

"It's a pleasure to meet you, Kalli." Her gaze landed on my lingerie, and she touched a piece of the silk. "Your designs are smart. Sexy yet elegant and classy."

"Everyone in town loves Kalli's designs," Lois said with a beaming smile. "I'm gonna surprise Mr. Flannigan for his birthday. You should buy one. Is there a special man in your life, Ms. Sinclaire?" Lois looked hopeful, as if she were waiting for Ms. Sinclaire to ask her to please call her Elouise.

That never happened.

"Who needs a man, darling? If I buy a piece of lingerie, it will be for myself. Men only cause problems."

"It's a shame what happened with the Bakers," Jaz said.

"Fay was a fool to marry Richard in the first place. It was only a matter of time before he cheated on her. He was weak. It didn't take much of a woman to sway him." Her eyes cut to mine. "No offense." This woman didn't even know me, but it was clear she was judging me by my looks.

"None taken. Ruby was nothing to me."

Elouise looked at me and tilted her head to the side. "Wasn't she your mother? You look just like her."

"No, she was my egg donor." I folded my hands in front of me. "I never knew her before she showed up in town out of the blue."

"Oh, well." She shrugged and went back to looking at clothes. "All I know is this divorce will be hard for Fay to overcome. People in our social circle can be so judgmental. They could care less about affairs until you get caught. It's why I'll never get married." She smiled slyly. "Don't get me wrong. I'm not anti-men. They serve their purpose, especially the handsome ones. I'm all for using them as escorts, among other things, but I'll never let one have the upper hand or gain control over me. My reputation is far more important to me than love."

"Fay really loved Richard," Lois said with a note of pity. "I feel so bad for her. She was devastated over his infidelity. I would be too if my Michael ever cheated on me. Like Fay and Richard, we don't have children. He's all I have."

Elouise shook her head sadly. "I really liked Fay, but she lost a lot of friends because of his betrayal and her filing for divorce. That kind of shunning can make a person go a little crazy." Elouise looked around and lowered her voice. "I'm a little worried about Fay. She vowed to get even with Ruby Winehouse if it was the last thing she did while we were at the charity auction, and a lot of people heard her. I was embarrassed for her."

"Well, someone certainly got even with Ruby," I said.

"How scandalous, and quite frankly, scary." It was clear Elouise loved gossip as much as Lois did. "And now her body is missing?" Elouise went on, her gray eyes growing wide. "How on earth does that even happen?"

"I don't know, but I'm sure we'll find out." I looked both women in the eyes to drive my point home. "If I've learned anything over the recent string of murders in Clearview, it's that the truth always comes out."

CHAPTER 11

"Hi, Kosmos, I'm here to pick up Jaz and my lunch order. We decided to eat in the shop today," I said to my cousin later that day. We were both behind on work because of the Harvest Festival and the murder investigation. I was in the middle of promoting my fall line for Interludes, but they would be looking for my winter collection designs soon.

I needed a little inspiration and a whole lot of caffeine.

"I've got you covered, Cuz." Kosmos handed the order to me while Silas rang me up. There were too many of us in town to give family members free food or discounts. No one would ever make a profit that way. I paid for our order and was about to leave.

"Hi, Kalli," a woman's voice said from behind me.

I turned around and saw Mable Griffith standing there, smiling shyly. She was in her usual slacks and sweater, her hair styled modestly and makeup light. I really didn't know her all that well, even though she had lived here for five years.

"Hi, Mable." I smiled back and looked beyond her

for Wally. They'd been spending a lot of time together since the bachelor auction. "Are you alone today?"

"Actually, I'm getting Wally and his staff's lunch order to go." A concerned look crossed her face. "I'm worried about him."

I quirked a brow. "How come?"

"He's taking it personally that Ruby's body went missing. He's very fond of your family and feels horrible that it happened on his watch."

I couldn't help but hold him somewhat responsible. If he'd had better security, that never would have happened. I didn't know how I felt about a lot of things at the moment. "I really can't understand how it happened, either," I finally replied. "The funeral home is on the outskirts of town, so I suppose that might make it easier for someone to escape with a body, but still. I can't imagine why anyone would want to steal a corpse."

"I don't know. With all these break-ins, maybe the person responsible thought Ruby might have whatever they were looking for on her person." Mable pursed her lips and wrinkled her brow. "I can tell you for certain, she didn't have anything in her clothes pockets or body cavities when I did her autopsy."

Well, that was a visual I couldn't erase.

I looked at my lunch and suddenly had no appetite. "I have no clue, but I'm worried we won't find her body in time to bury her."

"Unless the person put her on ice, she won't last long. And, unfortunately, even with refrigeration, time is of the essence."

"Well, I hope Wally and his staff enjoy their lunch." Because I certainly wouldn't be enjoying mine.

"I'm sure they will. They're getting sick of bringing packed lunches from what I hear. He won't let anyone leave to eat lunch out anymore, and he barely leaves at all himself. He's gotten even thinner than normal. If I don't bring lunch to him, then he won't eat."

"You're a good friend."

She shrugged, looking down. "I try."

I grabbed my bag and stepped out of her way so she could pay for her order. I was about to leave when Kosmos got a phone call. I knew my cousin well, and the look on his face didn't sit well with me. His skin tone had paled considerably.

"What's wrong, Kosmos?" I asked as soon as he hung up.

"I need to get to the hospital now," he said to me and Silas both, untying his apron. He was so tough and never vulnerable, but I saw his hands shake.

"Obviously, you're in no shape to drive, bro," Silas said. "Let me close up, and I'll drive you."

"We can't afford that." Kosmos grabbed his keys. His hands shook worse. Whatever it was, it had my normally unflappable cousin shook up. That was all it took for me to make a decision.

"Mable, will you drop off this lunch order to Jaz at Full Disclosure on your way to the Newcomer Funeral Home?"

"Absolutely." She took my order. "Do you want your salad?"

I was already shaking my head. "I'm not hungry, thanks. Just give the whole order to Jaz. I'm sure she'll eat it. And tell her I'll call her and explain soon."

Mable nodded. "I hope everything will be okay," she said to Kosmos who nodded his thanks as she left the diner.

"What happened?" I asked.

His gaze met mine. "That was the hospital.

Someone just ran Winnie's mail truck off the road, and apparently, she's hurt bad."

~

KOSMOS and I walked into Clearview Hospital and headed straight for the reception desk. He'd dated plenty of women, but I'd never seem him this affected by one. They'd only been on a few dates, but he was obviously the person she listed as an emergency contact. Her family still lived back in Australia, and apparently, she felt closest to him over everyone else in town.

"I'm here to see Winnie Wallaby," Kosmos said to the receptionist.

"Let's see. She's on floor three. You'll need to fill out this form and show your ID's, then we'll give you both a visitor's badge.

We did as she suggested, and then we took the elevator to the third floor and headed straight for the nurse's station. The second we stepped off the elevator, we were hit with cold air and the smell of antiseptic to keep the germs to a minimum.

Again, Kosmos asked to see Winnie.

"Have a seat in the waiting room. Doc LaLone is in there with her now," the nurse said with a neutral expression.

It was hard to get a read on her on how worried we needed to be.

"So, you and Winnie have grown pretty close, I take it." I sat down beside him and handed him the cup of horrible coffee I'd snagged from the vending machine.

"Thanks." He took a sip and winced. "Winnie's great. She's not like any other woman I've ever met."

"I can see that." I nudged him with my shoulder. "I never thought I'd see the day any woman could finally crack that big ole' heart of yours."

"I'm not like Silas." He lifted one shoulder. "I don't let people in very easily. I did that once when I was young."

"I remember." I squeezed his hand briefly. "I didn't think you would ever recover from Penelope breaking your heart."

"To be honest, neither did I." He set his jaw. "When I did finally get over her, I vowed never to let myself be vulnerable again." His face softened on a sigh. "A lot of good that did me. Look at me now?"

I looked at him in confusion. "But Winnie didn't break your heart."

"Not yet, but if I lose her, my heart will be torn to shreds." His gaze met mine. "I'm in love with her, and I haven't even had the chance to tell her yet."

"You have to stay positive. Don't put anything negative out into the universe. She's going to be okay. She has to be." I hugged him.

"I sure hope so," he said. *Or so help me Zeus, I'll kill the person who did this to her.*

My heart sank as I let go of him. That was all I needed. Another family member accused of murder. I said a little prayer and made the sign of the cross.

Just then Doc LaLone and Father Conery walked out of Winnie's room and joined us in the waiting room. Winnie was catholic, but usually a priest was only called in if the situation was grave. Sister Mary Margaret came barreling down the hall, saw us and slowed her pace as she joined them, folding her hands in front of her. Father looked at her with approval, if I wasn't mistaken. She *was* a lot younger than him, and clearly, he was trying to guide her.

Must be I wasn't the only one who saw that Sister Mary Margaret needed a little softening up.

Kosmos surged to his feet and shifted from side to side, wringing his hands.

"Kosmos." Doc nodded at him and then at me. "Kalli."

"It's good to see you again, Ms. Ballas." Father Conery smiled at me.

"Please, call me Kalli."

"As you wish."

"Nice to see you as well, Sister," I said, happy she was warming up.

She nodded her head demurely. "You as well, my child."

"I wish someone would tell me if Winnie is okay." Kosmos stood there with his hands clenched. "No offense, Father, I just can't take it anymore."

"None taken, my son." Father folded his hands in front of him. "It's good to see you again since mass."

My eyes sprang wide, but I didn't say a word.

Kosmos couldn't quite look at me. If his mama knew he went to a church other than our Greek Orthodox Church, heads would roll. She was about the only woman I'd ever seen Kosmos afraid of, and for good reason.

None of us messed with Aunt Irene.

Kosmos nodded to the priest and then looked at Doc in question. "Is she going to be okay?"

He'd just finished talking to the nurse and had turned back to us. "She's awake."

Kosmos started heading toward the door to her room, but Doc grabbed his arm. "You need to be prepared."

Kosmos nodded, unable to speak.

"Someone not only ran her off the road. They did

so with the intent to kill her by striking her on the edge of a cliff. Her mail truck flipped over several times. She was unconscious when she arrived here. Multiple lacerations, broken bones, and internal bleeding. She's lucky to be alive. I wasn't sure if she would wake up, but she has, and she's asking for you."

"Before you go, do you have any idea who might want to harm her?" Father Conery asked Kosmos.

"I can't imagine anyone wanting to harm Winnie." He frowned. "Although, she did say she felt like someone had been following her lately."

"She does deliver packages and letters to everyone in town, so she pretty much knows everyone's business," Doc pointed out.

"She did mention a package to Grayson Millbrook being damaged. He wasn't very happy with her, acting concerned she might have seen the contents inside. She assured him she didn't. And even if she did, it was her job to maintain confidentiality."

"Did she actually see what was inside?" I asked.

"I don't know, but I do know that even if she did, she would never tell me or anyone. She takes her job very seriously."

"I will pray for her safety and speedy healing," Father said.

"Thank you. I appreciate that. I'll ask Father Papadopoulos to as well." Kosmos looked at Doc. "Can we see her now?"

"Only one of you," Doc said. "And she specifically asked for you."

Kosmos hesitated and looked at me.

"Don't worry about me. I'm not going anywhere. I'll be here waiting for you when you're done."

He nodded once with obvious gratitude and emotion, then disappeared inside Winnie's room and closed the door, leaving me to wonder...

What the heck was in those packages, and was it worth killing over?

~

THAT NIGHT AT MY PARENTS' restaurant, Nik and I sat at a table in the far corner, eating gyros. My parents made the absolute best. We sat in comfortable silence, not needing words. There was never an awkward moment between us these days, but after the days we'd had, we didn't have the energy to put into finding a place that was super private.

We were running out of options.

"I can't believe what happened to Winnie." Nik tossed his napkin on the table as he sat back, looking as stuffed as I was. "It doesn't make sense. Why would someone want to run her off the road—scratch that, run her off a *cliff*—to the point of attempted murder?"

"Doc had a good point." I thought about the significance of what Doc LaLone had said. "Winnie delivers the mail and packages, so she sees what kind of mail and packages everyone in this town is getting. Then Kosmos pointed out that a package to Grayson was damaged, and he was angry at Winnie and suspected she saw what was inside."

"Interesting," Nik said. "Go on."

"Well, she tried to tell him she took her job very seriously and would always be discreet, but I guess he remained agitated."

"It does make you wonder what was inside that package," Nik said.

"Exactly. But like Doc said, many big players in

this town get packages. And I'm sure some of them are things they want kept private."

"Yeah, but how many people from out of town that are here for a festival are getting packages? If you're here on business, that's one thing. But here just for a festival and getting a package would seem suspicious to me."

"Agreed. I saw a package get delivered to Gary for Grayson at the hotel, as well. Maybe we can do some digging and find out more." I'd tried saying the same thing before, but no one had taken me seriously. I felt vindicated now that Detective Dreamy finally was.

"I'm on it."

"In the meantime, I need to visit the restroom. Order me some dessert."

He raised a brow. "I don't know how you have the room in that tiny frame of yours. I'm much bigger, and I can't eat another bite."

"I always have room for dessert. Organic, sugar free ones, anyway. Besides, I plan to bring my leftovers home." I grinned. "Ma will know what I like. I'll be back in a minute." I never used public restrooms, but Ma kept one stall out-of-order, when really it was sanitized and saved just for me.

"You got it." He winked, and my heart did a little flip.

I headed toward the back of the restaurant, feeling a little less stressed. Dating Nik wasn't distracting. It was actually helping me take my mind off my troubles. Jasper and Eleni were sitting at a cozy table for two, lost in conversation.

Thalia wasn't going to be too happy about that.

I kept walking, deciding I had enough on my plate to worry about. I was about to enter the restroom when I heard a noise down the hall. I could have sworn Ma was in the kitchen. Pop, too. Then who on earth was in her office?

I headed toward the door when the noise stopped. I stood still for several seconds, but the silence continued. Stepping forward, I was about to open the door when it suddenly swung wide, and someone stepped out.

Danny Ferrari.

We stared at each other in surprise, then he cleared his throat. "Wrong room." He towered over me, his dark buzz cut and tattoos intimidating.

I was through with being intimidated. I squared my shoulders and stood a little straighter. This was my parents' restaurant, and Nik was right in the dining room. I was safe.

"I should say so." I crossed my arms in front of me. "What were you doing in my parents' office?"

"Looking for the restroom." He didn't quite meet my gaze.

"Really?" I glanced above the door to the word OFFICE then down the hall to the clearly marked LADIES and GENTLEMEN doors, then back to him with a raised brow.

"Excuse me. I have to go. I'm expecting a delivery." He stepped past me and walked down the hall, ignoring the restrooms completely.

What did that mean? Snooping, lying, packages...oh, my.

Maybe we were looking in the wrong direction for the break-ins and the person who ran Winnie off the road and a possible drug dealer. Grayson Millbrook wasn't the only outsider looking guilty these days. And what on earth was so fascinating about my parents' office?

Danny Ferrari just became a lot more interesting.

CHAPTER 12

It was a Friday night, and as usual, Flannigan's Pub was hopping. The Irish pub had a singer playing guitar in the corner, with half the bar singing along. I'd donned a Fall sweater with a pencil skirt, heels, and I left my hair down. I glanced at my watch. Jaz was late like always. We were supposed to have a girls' night.

Jaz told me I needed one.

Eleni and Thalia reluctantly agreed to come but vowed not to speak to each other because of the whole Jasper love triangle. Jaz told them no man was worth fighting over. I was staying out of it. Meanwhile, I was the first one here.

I wiped off a stool three times and sat down.

"Well, there's my favorite cousin." Silas joined me at the bar moments later and sat on the stool next to me.

He flashed his famous dimples at the bartender, Zena Renner, who was now his girlfriend. For as tiny as she was, her personality was twice her size and her smile even bigger. She was the only woman who could hold her own against a flirt like Silas, but these days he saved his flirting for her alone. She poured him another round and added a glass of wine for me without even having to ask my order.

Apparently, Zena was part of the family already.

"Hey yourself." I smiled at my cousin, checking my glass for fingerprints or lipstick stains. Only when I was positive it was clean, did I take a sip.

"Let me guess. It's girls' night, and Jaz is late again." He nudged my shoulder teasingly, full of the devil, same as always.

I nudged him back. "You got it. Thalia and Eleni are late, too. I'm actually surprised they agreed to be in the same room together."

"I heard. Man, it's tough dating in today's world."

"Oh, please, not long ago you thrived in it."

"That was before I found Zena." His gaze traveled down the bar, and she looked at him as if she felt his magnetism.

She blew him a kiss while making drinks, not missing a beat.

"She's really good," I said, impressed. "Michael Flannigan was a smart man to hire someone like her."

"She's the best." His voice rang with pride.

"I'm happy for you. I like seeing you settled down a bit."

"You could be, too, Kal," Silas said in a rare moment of seriousness. "It's not so bad. Nik is a great guy."

"Yup, he is." I swirled my wine around in my glass, not knowing what to say because I wasn't really sure what my problem was to begin with, other than paralyzing fear. "How's Kosmos?" I changed the subject to safer territory.

Silas peeled the label from his beer bottle. "He's at the hospital constantly. I mean, I get it. I would be there, too, if anything ever happened to Zena. But I worry about him. He's not eating or sleeping well."

"I thought Winnie was getting better?"

"She is, but you never know if things might take a turn for the worse with internal injuries. Her healing is going to take a long time."

"Are you worried about the diner?"

"Nah, you know how the family is. Everyone has stepped up and pitched in to help. I just want my brother back. And if Winnie does take a turn for the worse, I don't think Kosmos would recover this time. This would be much worse than the Penelope situation."

"That's why love isn't worth it." Thalia joined us at the bar on my other side. She already had a dirty martini in her hand. Her eyes were full of cynicism and disappointment as she took a big sip.

"You just haven't found the right guy." Silas grinned. "A guy like me."

And he's back, I thought with a little smile.

"Yeah, that's my problem. I've always wanted to date a guy like you, Cuz." Thalia rolled her eyes, then focused on me. "Where's Jaz?"

"Late. So's Eleni." I took another sip of my wine, then patted my lips dry three times with the sanitized cocktail napkin I'd brought with me

"Mmmm," was all Thalia said.

"Speaking of single," Silas jumped back in, "the Creed brothers are here." He pointed to the far side of the bar.

"The cleaning crew company?" I followed his gaze across the bar to where the three brothers sat.

The men were all blond haired, blue eyed, short and muscular. The brothers were handsome enough, but not exactly Thalia's type. She preferred tall, dark and handsome. Basically, men like Jasper.

"I don't want to date anyone," Thalia replied, going beyond my suspicions about the brother's not being her type.

It sounded like she'd sworn off men altogether. I couldn't blame her. Men were complicated. *Dating* was complicated. Add to that my quirks and my mind reading ability, and I was pretty much in stress over-load twenty-four seven.

"Dating is overrated." Eleni joined us, yanking me from my thoughts. She looked at Thalia and raised her glass. "Just saying."

Thalia lifted a brow, studied her for a moment, then raised her martini glass and clinked it against Eleni's Cosmopolitan.

And just like that, their feud was over.

"So sorry I'm late." Jaz finally joined us. "It took me forever to get the pups to settle down for Boomer."

"Well, at least you're here now," I said.

I looked over at the Creed brothers and blinked. Grayson and Elouise were talking with them. Together. Were they on a date? Grayson sure made the rounds. I had thought he was into Tammy. Even more confusing is what were they doing talking to the Creed brothers? I had to find out what they were up to.

Grayson and Elouise left together, looking pretty chummy.

"I'll be right back. I'm going to use the restroom," I added. "Save my place."

"Okay." Jaz looked at me in surprise and then sus-picion as she sat on my stool and ordered a drink. She was my best friend. She knew I didn't use public re-strooms, but she also kept all my secrets even if she didn't know what they were for sure.

I headed for the restroom and stopped by a table on the way. "Hi, guys," I said to Calvin, Caleb, and Christopher Crew.

They had a pitcher of beer in the center of their table with one extra chair. "Hey, Kalli, have a seat," Christopher said.

"Yes, join us," Caleb seconded.

"Maybe for just a moment." I wiped off the seat and then sat. Pretty much everyone in town knew about my quirks, so why bother hiding them?

"Would you like a glass of beer?" Calvin asked.

"Oh, no thank you. I can only stay for a moment. My girls are waiting for me at the bar." I pointed to the stools they sat on.

The brother's faces lit up. "We can make room if they'd like to join us," Christopher said, his eyes growing big with excitement.

"Oh, that's okay. They prefer sitting at the bar." I felt bad, but Thalia had already expressed her lack of interest. And now that Eleni wasn't dating Jasper either, I was pretty sure neither of them were big on men at the moment.

"Oh." Calvin's face registered his disappointment as well.

"So, what's up?" Caleb puckered his forehead. "You're still dating Detective Stevens, right?"

"Yes." I left off the part that we weren't official yet because I didn't want to get their hopes up over me, either.

"Oh, well then, did you stop by for another reason?" He looked concerned. "Are your parents satisfied with our work at Aphrodite's?"

"They're thrilled," I reassured them. "They love your work. I stopped by your table because I noticed Garyson Millbrook and Elouise Sinclaire talking to you earlier. Do you mind if I ask you what they were talking about?"

"I don't see why not." Christopher shrugged.

"I know Nik already talked to you about cleaning Newcomer Funeral Home and having access to a key. You guys were at the Clearview Motel on that day, so you're cleared of any suspicion. However, Grayson Millbrook has *not* been cleared, so I'm curious as to what he wanted from you."

"It was kind of weird. He wanted to know if we cleaned Ruby's room after she died," Caleb said.

"Did you?" I asked.

"Yes, and he wanted to know if we found anything unusual," Calvin answered. "Everyone says he had a thing for Ruby, but this seemed different. Like he was prying into her life for some other reason."

"Interesting. Found anything unusual like what?"

"He wouldn't say," Christopher chimed in.

"What was Elouise doing while this conversation was happening?"

"Drinking and flirting with Grayson. She could care less about us," Caleb said. "She was trying to hurry Grayson along so they could leave."

"I think she was looking forward to the rest of their evening alone," Calvin added with a snort.

"Well, thank you, boys. You've been a help. I'd better get going." I stood up and started to step away from the table.

"Put in a good word for us?" Christopher wore a hopeful puppy dog expression I couldn't risk disappointing.

"Sure thing." I smiled and left, wondering could Grayson have been interested in Ruby for more than just romance? If so, what could the reason have been.

Most importantly, what exactly had he been hoping to find in her room?

~

THE NEXT MORNING Nik and I decided to go to Sinfully Delicious before leaving for work. There was a line, so we talked while we waited to place our orders, the smell of cinnamon and nutmeg making my mouth water.

"So, how was last night?" Nik asked. "Did you have fun?"

"I did." I looked up at him. "But I missed you."

"Really now?" The corners of his eyes crinkled as his lips tipped up a little.

"Thalia and Eleni made up," I added.

He let out a big breath. "That's good to hear. I hate to see my cousin unhappy. Yours either." He puckered his forehead. "So, no more Jasper?"

"I guess he's just passing through Clearview. Making some money doing odd jobs but hasn't found a place to call home yet."

"He's a little quiet, but he seems like a decent guy from what I gather. I think he's helped just about everyone in town out."

"Thalia said he moves around a lot. And Eleni said he had a rough childhood, in and out of foster homes since the age of five and then on his own since eighteen."

"That's rough."

"Yeah, he said we're lucky to have our big Greek families." I rolled my head on my shoulders, trying to ease the knots in my neck. "I have to say through all of this stuff that happened with Ruby, I couldn't agree with Jasper more. I have a newfound appreciation for

Ma and Pop. They gave me such an amazing life. Sometimes I think I take that for granted. I don't mean to, but it's easy to do when you've never had to suffer."

"That's true. My ma is great, and even my pop. She might not like him, but we still have a good relationship. I just don't get to see him a lot since he lives across the pond. I've been thinking about taking a trip there when things slow down a bit." His gaze met and held mine. "Maybe you'll go with me."

"Maybe," I said, but just thinking about being confined in an airplane with germs floating around me had my heart skipping a beat. "Oh, look, it's our turn."

He didn't say another word. We stepped up and placed our orders to Maria's staff then stepped to the pickup side to wait. I looked at the back of the line when the door chimed as it opened. Father Conery, Sister Mary Margaret, and Danny all walked in together, talking.

"What do you think Danny is doing with Father Conery?"

Nik glanced over his shoulder, looking pensive. "Well, Ferrari is Italian. Maybe he's Catholic. If so, then it wouldn't be out of the ordinary that he'd be talking to a catholic priest and nun."

"He's another one I can't figure out," I said.

"How so?"

"Well, he's in town for the Harvest Festival, yet I never see him there. Gary said he's always gone from the Motel. Where does he spend his time? I've seen him out at a few restaurants, and I still catch him watching me with a funny look. And then there's the time he was in Ma's office, claiming he was looking for the bathrooms. I don't believe that for a second. They're clearly marked."

"Maybe he wasn't looking up. Many people are on

their phones and distracted these days. Do you know how many people get hit by cars because they walk while checking their phones?" Nik shook his head. "It's a sad reality."

"Maybe, but when I questioned him, he said he had to go. That he was expecting a package. And then he walked right by the real bathroom, never using it. He just seems suspicious to me."

"Who knows." Nik shrugged. "Like Grayson, maybe he's conducting business while he's here. We really don't have much to go on as far as he's concerned, so we can't pry into his business without just cause."

"I don't know. I just keep getting this feeling that he's up to no good. Maybe with Vinny or maybe he's linked to Grayson. Maybe he's the one doing the break-ins. He certainly looks scary enough to be a thug."

"You watch too many crime movies, Ballas." He tweaked my nose.

"Maybe so, Detective, but I'd still feel better if you'd keep an eye on him." I poked him in the chest.

"If it will make you feel better, then I will."

"Good. Also, Elouise said men were worthless, yet she was with Grayson. Last I knew, Grayson was with Tammy. And why was Grayson asking Creed's Cleaning Crew about Ruby's room and if they found anything unusual after her death?"

"All good questions I'll look into. Our order's ready, so I guess I'll go do my job." He grabbed his and Boomer's order, sliding mine in front of me. "And you do your job, please. No more playing detective."

"Cross my heart." I gave him a quick kiss and then placed a hand over my chest, but he didn't see the fingers I had crossed behind my back.

CHAPTER 13

At the end of the day, I stopped into my Aunt Tasoula's hair salon with Jaz. I always loved the smells of hair products and makeup. My aunt kept a special sanitized pink cape just for me in the back, but I wasn't here to get my hair cut. Ma told me my aunt wanted dinner dropped off. She had some big plans that were hush hush.

Something about having no privacy in this town of Ballas and Pagonis families.

My aunt was expanding by adding a nail technician and an aesthetician. Jasper stepped out from the back room, spotted us and couldn't quite make eye contact, then he headed over to talk to my aunt on the other side of the room.

But not so far that we couldn't hear what he was saying.

"I finished installing the bed for the facial procedures and the nail tech chair," he said, adding, "There's a problem with one of the sinks leaking. Once I finish that, you'll be good to go."

"Oh, okay. You such a nice boy. Too bad you no

Greek." She squeezed his cheeks then patted his face and let go on a trilling laugh.

"I wish I were Greek. You have a great family." The sincerity in his voice and expression on his face was unmistakable. "Is there anything else I can do for you before I go, Mrs. Chaconas?"

Legally, my Aunt Tasoula's name was still that of her late husband's, Leon Chaconas, but she mostly went by Tasoula or Ms. Ballas. I once told her that her name wasn't legally Ballas anymore.

She said, "Legal, schmegal, I'll always be a Ballas." And she pretty much had been ever since. She'd never liked the name Chaconas. Said it was too close to ca-hones and nothing good had ever come of those except her only son and grandson.

"You call me Aunt Tasoula, ya?" She nodded on a grin.

"I'd be honored," Jasper said with a rare smile.

"Now you set up my pole so I can tease the strip, okay? Okay." She patted his face again and walked away.

Jasper stood there scratching his head for a long minute, then shrugged and walked to the front of the salon.

Jaz looked at me with wide eyes. "She didn't."

I looked around, my eyes landing on something I never thought I would see in my aunt's hair salon, or any of my family's businesses. A long, gold-plated pole with two big plates on each end leaning against the wall in the corner of the Hera's Halo waiting room.

"Oh, yes, she did." I pointed.

Jasper spotted the pole and then got to work, obviously learning to speak *Tasoula* pretty quickly.

I marched over to my aunt. "Aunt Tasoula, what are you doing with a stripper pole in your hair salon?"

"Well, hello to you, too," she said with a sarcastic tone as she clipped away, trimming Fay Baker's hair and humming showtunes.

I suddenly had a vision of the Pink Ladies on the stage at Pearl's Place and squeezed my eyes shut for a minute. I couldn't unsee what I already saw, and I feared my mind had burned the image into my brain. I wondered if any brain cells could be damaged from a burned image. Shaking off that disturbing thought, I waved to Fay.

She barely looked at me and nodded stiffly, then went back to her magazine.

I frowned. What had I done to her?

Sighing, I replied to my aunt, "Hi yourself," then I kissed her cheek. "Ma sent us with dinner for you. She said you requested it and had big plans." I waited on bated breath, curious about what my aunt planned to do in her salon after closing.

"Did she tell you about my renovations to my back room?" She glossed right over my comment, keeping me dying in the dark as she clipped away.

"Yes. It sounds like a great use of the space." I personally didn't like anyone touching my feet or hands, and no one was poking needles into my face or injecting foreign substances into my skin. No amount of wrinkles would be worth the side effects that could come along with those procedures. "Jaz tagged along to check it out as well. She's super excited. This is more up her alley than mine."

"This is definitely up my alley. Things must be going well for you," Jaz said, looking around with excitement shining in her eyes. "I can't wait to check out your new services. When will they start?"

"Smart woman. They'll start soon. Tell your friends."

"I certainly will."

"So, about the stripper pole...?" I asked again less aggressively, hoping she would spill the beans.

"Dancing the pole is like teasing the strip. You burn lots of calories without having to take your clothes off. Win win."

"I've heard pole dancing burns a lot of calories," Jaz said.

"And increases the metabolic syndrome."

"Metabolism?" I asked.

"That's what I said," she went on. "It balance the muscle and flex the tone. Men like the core strong. I know these things."

"How do you know what size to get?" Jaz glanced over to watch Jasper work on putting the pole together.

"It goes tall or short. Spinny or still. You no can be over five hundred pounds, though. Or you breaka the pole."

"Don't even think about putting one of those in Full Disclosure." I stared at Jaz, appalled at the thought.

"Why not?" Aunt Tasoula said. "I bet you sell more naughty nighties that way. It's true. You'll see."

"There's nothing naughty about my nighties, and I sell plenty of my designs without a stripper pole, thank you very much. I'm going for classy not trashy."

I shuddered to think of the clientele we would get with having a stripper pole in Full Disclosure. Our store was all about elegance and class. My loft was my happy place where I found inspiration for my designs. I did not want it tainted by people teasing the strip or anything else for that matter.

"What on earth are you trying to sell by installing

one in your hair salon?" I finally asked, almost afraid
to hear the answer.

"I'm not *selling* anything, Ms. Prude." Aunt Tasoula
shrugged. "I work long hours. This way my stone kills
two birds."

Jaz looked at her in horror, needing Babble to keep
up with the Tasoula language. The lingo changed
daily.

"I exercise on my breaks between work," Aunt
Tasoula went on oblivious. "Win Win." She grinned.

"Is it open to your customers to use?" Fay lowered
her magazine with interest in us finally. "Apparently,
pole dancing is what men like."

"Of course. My customers can dance the pole
while they wait, but no teasing the strip in my shop.
Only me." She slapped her chest.

I gaped at her.

"What? With blinds down after hours, of course."
She looked at her watch. "Speaking of after hours.
Tate Hemsworth should be here soon." The bell over
the door chimed, but Tate was *not* the man who
walked through the door.

Richard Baker and Grayson Millbrook walked inside together.

Jaz and I looked at each other, ready to call the police if necessary.

"Richard, what are you doing here?" Fay seemed a
lot less uppity and a lot more flustered than she had
moments before.

"I came to see you here since you won't return my
calls." Richard's clothes were rumpled, and his hair
was a mess. He looked like he hadn't slept in days.

"You no harass my clients here." Aunt Tasoula
swiped her hand through the air with her scissors, no
police necessary.

"You heard the lady," Fay said.

"I'm not trying to harass my wife," Richard replied to my aunt, then looked back at Fay. "I'm trying to beg her to forgive me."

"You bad boy. Real men know how to treat a lady." This time Aunt Tasoula's comb sliced through the air. "She no forgive."

"Well, she *maybe* forgive." Fay lifted one shoulder on a whine. "It's really hard to get divorced and still have friends in this town."

"Wait." Richard's eyes filled with hope. "Are you saying what I think you're saying, babe?"

"I'm not sure yet." She pouted. "You humiliated me. I couldn't show my face anywhere without having everyone look at me with pity."

"I promise you won't regret it." Richard dropped to one knee next to her chair and pulled out a ring box.

He either walked around with that all the time in hopes of catching Fay in a vulnerable moment like this, or he knew she would say yes. These people were so phony. They only cared about their image and social standing.

"Let's renew our vows. I will spend the rest of our lives making it up to you. No one even remembers that woman's name anymore. I promise you."

That woman.

I just sat there numb, staring at them as they talked about Ruby right in front of me as if she were nothing. Nobody. I didn't know her, but she was my biological mother, and she had been murdered. She was a human being, after all.

I didn't know what to feel.

"Yes!" Fay clapped her hands, startling me when she finally answered his proposal. "I can't wait to plan the party of the year and invite all our friends. It will be the perfect way back into society."

"Are you okay?" Jaz stood beside me with a knowing expression on her face. She'd heard everything that I'd heard and looked just as shocked.

I nodded but didn't speak.

"I'm finished, Tasoula." Jasper came to a stop beside us and studied me. "Everything okay over here, ladies?"

"I'm fine," I managed to say.

Jasper nodded once to me, gave the Bakers a dirty look, said goodbye to my aunt and then walked out of the salon.

"Why wouldn't you be fine?" Richard said, finally tuning in to what was happening around him.

"That woman was her mother." Fay gave me a disgusted look. "Can't you tell just by looking at her? She looks just like the tramp. Her adoptive mother did us all a favor by getting rid of the trash."

"Have you seen my man? He's a big one." Aunt Tasoula whipped the cape off of Fay with her hair only half cut. "You no say another word about my niece *or* my sister. Do I make myself clear?"

"Well, I never." Fay stood up.

Aunt Tasoula looked her up and down and then snorted. "A scrawny thing like you with no meat on your bones? I no surprised." She spit and tossed some salt over her shoulder. "Now get out."

"Don't you spit on me!"

"You no try to give me The Evil Eye! Amateur."

"The evil what? You're crazy. You'll regret treating me this way." Fay stuck her nose in the air. "Do you know who I am? I can ruin you."

Aunt Tasoula laughed in her face. "Do *you* know who *I* am? My family owns this town. I can blacklist you, and you no get your hair fixed again. You play nice, I only make you suffer one week. Now run along, little girl, before I really get mad."

Richard took a dumbfounded Fay by the arm, glared at Aunt Tasoula and me, then looked at Grayson in question. "You coming?"

Grayson eyed Aunt Tasoula with interest. "No, I don't believe I will."

"And *you* will regret that," Richard ground out. "Just remember what we talked about, and we'll be square."

Grayson didn't say anything, but his body was stiff as he watched Richard and Fay Baker leave the salon.

"What was that about?" I asked.

His gaze met mine and held as he studied me intensely before replying, "Business," and then looking away. "Would you care to have dinner with me, Ms. Ballas?" Grayson asked my aunt gallantly, practically bowing at her feet.

"Me?" Aunt Tasoula blinked at Grayson in surprise. "Why?" She was a good decade older than him.

"Why not? You're quite a woman. I imagine it would take quite a man to keep up with you," Grayson's voice lowered seductively.

"Oh, go on with you now," Aunt Tasoula said, her cheeks flushing pink. "No, really. Go on." She twirled her hand in circles. "Tell me more."

My jaw unhinged.

"I'll tell you more," a deep male voice said as he walked through the open door. "The lady has plans tonight if I'm not mistaken." Tate Hemsworth glared at Grayson and then grinned devilishly at my aunt.

"Oh, I most definitely have plans tonight." Aunt Tasoula winked then looked at Grayson. "I told you he was big."

"Another time, then." Grayson tipped his head to my aunt, ignored Tate, then met my gaze intensely one last time before leaving.

I felt the same feeling course through me as I did when I was being watched.

"Okay, shoo shoo," my aunt said to me, ushering Jaz and myself to the door. "It's closing time, and I have big plans. Thank Ophelia for the food." She shut the door before I could say another word.

And then closed the blinds.

CHAPTER 14

I walked into the catholic church, St. Rose of Lima, feeling peaceful yet guilty. It wasn't my church, and I didn't want Ma to worry I was converting. I loved my church, and Father Papadopoulos had relented early, finally letting the mamas back in.

Even Agnes was behaving herself, and the choir had never sounded better.

But there was something calming about this catholic church today. I couldn't explain why and didn't quite understand it, but I welcomed it after all the stress I had been under lately. Maybe it was because I still felt like someone was watching me everywhere I went, yet in here, I felt safe.

But that wasn't why I had come here today.

I wanted to speak with Father Conery about Grayson. I'd seen them together a few times now. The Harvest Festival was over. Ruby was still missing. He didn't act like a grieving man. In fact, he seemed like a player, yet he never stayed with anyone for long.

So why was he still in Clearview?

I walked to the front of the church and sat in the first pew. Church wasn't in session. I heard a maintenance man off to the side, humming eighties rock music as he worked on the heating unit now that the days were growing colder.

Creed's Cleaning Crew was here as well. I'd seen their van out back. Noises like a vacuum cleaner were coming from the basement, so they were probably cleaning the religious education and preschool classrooms.

I folded my hands and closed my eyes, then did some deep breathing and meditating. Taking advantage of the calmness I felt, I tried to ground myself. Just when I felt centered and less stressed, a noise up on the altar jolted me.

My eyes whipped open to see Danny Ferrari exiting the confessional booth.

He stepped down from the altar, stumbled a moment when he saw me, then picked up the pace. He nodded once as he passed by me, muttering hello, then he left without saying another word or making eye contact. What had he been confessing? Murder? Burglary? Stalking? I didn't trust him.

There was definitely something about him he didn't want me to know.

A few minutes later, Father Conery emerged from the confessional. Sister Mary Margaret scurried over to him, and they were talking for several moments, her hands moving as fast as Ma's when she talked.

After a minute, they spotted me.

Sister straightened her spine, stilled her movements, then nodded to me demurely. She calmly turned around to slowly walk away. Father looked in my direction and smiled kindly. He made his way down the aisle to the pew I sat in.

"May I join you, Ms. Ballas?"

"Certainly, Father, but please call me Kalli. Is

Sister Mary Margaret okay? She seems a little frazzled."

"She's fine. Changing a parish even temporarily is an adjustment for the parishioners as well as the priests and nuns. She's adapting with my help."

"She's lucky to have you. The whole parish is. How is Father Comstock since his surgery?"

"His recovery isn't going as smoothly as anyone had hoped." Father Conery looked concerned. "I'm not sure when or if he'll be back. Obviously, Sister and I will stay as long as the parish needs us."

"Poor Father. I'll have Ma make him some soup."

"I'm sure he would enjoy that."

"In the meantime, let me know if you or Sister need anything at all. I'm at your disposal and happy to assist."

He tilted his head and studied me with all seeing eyes. "The greater question is what can I do for you? What troubles you this evening, child?"

"Me?" It was uncanny how men and women of the cloth could sense a person in need before the person spoke a single word. "Oh, nothing, really. I just have a few questions I would like to ask you if you don't mind."

"The questions can wait. I can see something is bothering you. I know you have your own church and Father Papadopoulos, but I want you to know I'm here for you as well. I'm a good listener for what it's worth."

I sat there for a moment, thinking this could be a real opportunity for me to get things off my chest, and the words started coming out of my mouth as if they had a will of their own. "It's just the whole thing with Ruby? I know I can tell Father Papadopoulos, but with Ma being accused of her murder and talking to him, too, it's just hard to open up fully. No offense, but you're an outsider. I feel like you're the only one who can be truly impartial."

"I'm listening."

"Ma is the only mother I've ever known. She adopted me right after I was born. I occasionally thought about who my birth parents might be and why they gave me up, but only briefly. I've had a blessed life."

"That's wonderful."

"Yes, it was, until out of the blue, this woman shows up claiming to be my biological mother. There's no denying it. I look exactly like her. She tells me I'm like my biological father, and then I find out he used to be her drug dealer. They were together only one time, and then he split. I guess I take after him with my quirks, so I kind of get how he couldn't handle that part."

"Not everyone is meant to be a parent."

"That's true. I often worry maybe I'm not meant to be one, either. The only reason I can handle being close to a man is because I can read minds. Trust me when I say Detective Stevens' thoughts make me forget everything else." I peeked up at Father Conery.

He didn't so much as blink. He just kept looking at me calmly, patiently waiting for me to continue.

I let out a huge breath, so grateful to have told at least one person other than Jaz about my gift. "After a freak fall and hitting my head, I can suddenly hear what other people are thinking, but only when touching them." I shuddered. "Imagine how hard that is for an OCD germaphobe like me."

His lips tipped up a little, and he continued to listen.

"Anyway, the guy I'm dating, Detective Nikos Stevens, wants to make our relationship official. I'm worried about ruining what we have. I'm worried he'll think I'm a freak if he finds out about my gift. I'm worried my gift will go away, and I won't be able to be with him like I am now anymore." I sighed. "I'm just worried."

"It's okay to worry, so long as you don't let it gain control over your life." He spoke as if from experience.

"Easier said than done, Father. As for my birth mother, I'm not sure how I'm supposed to feel. I met her, found out she only wanted money from me, and then she was murdered. Suddenly, I'm her only next of kin and responsible for her body, only to have her vanish. I still can't wrap my mind around how that could happen."

"It is a mystery for sure."

"On top of all that, Ma is still the number one suspect in Ruby's murder investigation. So, I'm pretty much avoiding relationship convos while losing my mind with worry over Ma and trying to solve a murder all at the same time. So, that's what's bothering me, Father. Aren't you glad you asked?"

He sat there for several minutes, and I thought maybe he wasn't going to speak. He'd probably never had to help someone quite like me and maybe didn't know what to say. I didn't blame him. I could be a lot to handle on a good day.

"Here are my thoughts. Your mother couldn't have been too horrible. She chose to give you life and give you up to a family she knew could do far better for you than she could. It's been a long time since your birth. She's most likely had a tough time of things."

"Other people have tough times, but they don't become bad people."

"That's true, but life can change a person for the good or bad. If you don't let go of your anger and forgive her, you'll never be able to move forward with your own life." He let his words sink in and then looked me in the eye. "Just because this horrible thing has happened to her, it's not your fault. You can't blame yourself for things you can't control."

A lump filled my throat. I had been blaming myself. Taking a deep breath, a weight lifted off my shoulders. It wasn't my fault Ruby gave me up just like it wasn't my fault that she died and went missing.

"As for your father," the priest continued, "it sounds like he wasn't equipped to be a parent any more than she was." He smiled fondly. "You have a wonderful family who loves you. Cherish that."

I sat there listening to him talk and digesting what he had to say.

"As for this gift of yours." He studied me with a mixture of curiosity and fascination. "The Lord works in mysterious ways. He obviously gave you this ability for a reason. It's what you choose to do with it that's important."

"Thank you for not thinking I'm crazy."

"Who says I don't." He chuckled. "Aren't we all a little bit?" His face grew serious. "Don't squander this ability. Use it to help others."

I was already nodding. "That's what I'm trying to do each time I help solve a murder. I just want to do my part and make a difference."

He nodded. "That's good. And as for this detective of yours. If I've learned anything over the years, it's that life is short and precious. You don't want to live with regrets. What do you have to lose if you try? Nothing. If it doesn't work, then it doesn't work, and at least you know. But if you never try, you lose for sure. You might miss out on something wonderful. Don't let fear of the unknown hold you back, Kalli."

"You make some good points, Father."

"And tell your detective the truth. Nothing good comes from a lie. If he can accept you with quirks, gifts, and all, then you know you have something special."

"You're right." I inhaled a deep breath. "I just have to figure out when and how."

"Good girl." He rubbed his hands together. "Okay, so now for your questions?"

"I saw Danny Ferrari coming out of your confessional, so I know that he's catholic." I help up my hand before Father said a word. "I know you can't tell me what he said. I was just confirming he's catholic." I pursed my brow. "What about Grayson Millbrook? Is he catholic as well?"

"Not that I know of. Why?"

"I've seen you two together a couple times now."

"I don't just talk to catholic people, you know."

"I know, I just have a bad feeling about him. Danny, too. Do you think they're dangerous people?"

Father frowned. "That's a good question. I think all of us are capable of many things if pushed hard enough. Even murder."

~

AFTER I LEFT THE CHURCH, I drove straight home, feeling vulnerable and drained. I knew Father Conery was right. I had to tell Nik about my gift, and one day I would. I just wasn't sure when. Definitely not before this murder investigation was over with, and Ma's name was officially cleared.

I also knew anything worth having was worth fighting for.

I didn't want to go through life with regrets, wondering what if Nik and I could have worked out. Father was right. If I didn't at least try, then I would never know for sure. And I needed to forgive my birth parents. Not for them, but for me. So, I could move on to the next chapter of my life.

Dark clouds rolled in, obliterating what little light was left. The wind picked up and swirled leaves in mini cyclones across the road. The first fat raindrops began to fall. It was going to be a doozy of a storm.

I hated driving in bad weather. The risk of my Prius hydroplaning or blowing a tire had my pulse kicking into overdrive. The raindrops turned into a torrential downpour. My wipers were on high, and it was like I was in a carwash. I couldn't see a thing.

Somehow, I made it home alive.

I pulled into my half of the driveway, but Nik wasn't home yet. I waited a beat for it to let up, but it never did. Grabbing my tote bag that contained my design samples, purse, hand sanitizer and anything else I might possibly need, I made a mad dash to my front door. After what felt like forever, I finally made it safely inside.

Ms. Priss gave me a look, and I wondered if animals could give a person The Evil Eye as well. If so, then I was pretty sure she cursed me on a daily basis.

"You're such a spoiled princess." I set my tote bag on the matt by the front door, then slipped off my wet shoes and set them on the boot tray. Taking off my coat, I hung it on the coat rack, and then finally made my way to the kitchen.

I put my cat's food in her fancy food dish and then went into my bedroom to change out of my wet clothes. Donning my usual yoga pants, a fleece sweatshirt, and warm socks, I let my hair down from its usual bun and rubbed my aching scalp. Now the most difficult question of the night....

What to make for dinner?

Walking back into the kitchen, I looked down and noticed Prissy's full food dish. Usually, she ate her food immediately. My gut twisted into knots. What if she was sick? Father was right. Life was short and precious. I couldn't imagine what life would be like without my precious Prissy in it.

"Here, kitty kitty," I said, walking around the entire half of my house, looking in every room.

Where on earth had she gone?

I was about to check under beds, in drawers, in closets and anywhere a cat could possibly hide, when I saw a movement outside the sliding door to my deck. Ms. Priss stood outside in the pouring rain, looking miserable and definitely not happy with me.

Oh, I was being cursed for sure.

"How in the world did you get out there?" I opened the door to let her back in. She shook everywhere, her calico fur flinging water at me. I would need another shower. The pollutants in rainwater could be harmful to my skin. I turned around to head straight to my bathroom but froze in my tracks and screamed for all I was worth.

Prissy hissed and bolted from the room.

A person stood before me, dressed all in black with a mask on and gloves. Everything happened so fast. It was impossible to tell if it was a man or woman, and I didn't have a chance to take in any details because they wrapped their hands around my neck and squeezed. A sliver of skin between their glove and shirt touched my collarbone.

Where is it? You have to know something. I know you do.

I tried to shake my head no, and the connection of skin-on-skin was lost. I couldn't move. The voice was a neutral hiss. Again, impossible to tell if it came from a male or a female. All the self-defense training I had learned went straight out the window to be washed away in the deluge happening off my deck.

I squirmed and kicked and clawed my way to no avail. The world around me started to grow dark and narrow to tunnel vision. I had to break free. Air. I needed air. I couldn't die like this. Die at the hands of the same person who killed my birth mother.

All I could think about was I never got a chance to tell Nik how I really felt.

From some far away part of my brain, I registered hearing a noise outside like a car door closing followed by the bark of a dog. Could Nik be home? Wolfgang? If only I could let them know I needed help. But it was too late for me.

The room spun and faded to black.

CHAPTER 15

"**Y**ou're very lucky," Doc LaLone said from the exam room in his office.

His white lab coat looked as pristine as ever because his wife Joan, who was also his nurse, kept it that way, and his stethoscope hung loose around his neck. His daughter Cindy was his receptionist, but tonight, we were the only ones in the building. Doc didn't usually hold evening hours, but when Nik called him, he met him at his office just for me.

"Believe me, I know," I responded, my voice sounding hoarse.

"Don't talk," Nik chimed in, his clothes a total wrinkled mess and hair standing out all over the place from the rain.

"Detective Stevens got home just in time. A minute longer, and your assailant would have crushed your windpipe, or worse," Doc met my eyes to let his meaning sink in, "finished strangling you."

My fingers fluttered to the bruises in the shape of fingers that surrounded my throat. The person kept moving their hands, so the marks were blurred together, making it impossible to tell if my attacker had been big or small.

"I'm just glad I got home when I did. There was no sign of a break-in. I was planning on going home and eating my take-out, but Wolfgang sprinted to Kalli's door and growled. That was all it took. I dropped my food, drew my weapon, and raced inside."

"Thank the gods." I shivered over the thought of what would have happened if my boy Wolfy hadn't growled.

I owed him several pets and maybe even a kiss.

A muscle in Nik's jaw bulged, and I could feel his anger emanating off him in deadly waves as he continued. "The slider was open, and the person was gone, leaving Kalli lying in an unconscious heap on the floor." He closed his eyes for a moment and swallowed hard, his Adam's apple bobbing once. "I thought I'd lost her." He looked at me. "I really thought you were already dead."

"So did I." I took a sip of the water that Doc had handed me. It hurt to swallow. "Hearing you call my name, and then opening my eyes and seeing your face was nothing short of a miracle to me."

"You have no idea how I felt when you suddenly looked at me with a wide, terror filled gaze." Nik's eyes filled with moisture, and he didn't even try to hide it, which just made me like him even more.

"Do you have any idea what your attacker wanted?" Doc asked.

"To kill her," Nik growled then looked at me so intensely. "Are you sure you couldn't tell if it was a man or a woman? Any distinct marks? Tattoos? Anything at all that might identify the person?" I knew he was desperate to find this person even more than he would normally be because I was the victim.

"No. It happened so fast. I was just trying to stay alive. Their body was completely covered in black, and the voice husky and disguised, more like a hiss. I wish I could remember more. I'm going to be looking over my shoulder suspiciously at everyone."

"I'm not going to let you out of my sight." Nik grunted.

I smiled tenderly. "Also, I think the person wanted more than to kill me. I think he or she was looking for something specific."

"What makes you think that? Nothing was ransacked like the other break-ins." Nik's brow furrowed in concentration.

"I think I surprised the person and got home before they had a chance to trash my place." The thought of someone touching my personal things was unbearable. The first chance I had, I planned to sterilize my entire half of the house. "Anyway, I heard them think...I mean say...*Where is it? You have to know something. I know you do.*" I shook my head. "I've never felt someone so full of rage before. I think their anger and frustration overtook their desire to find whatever they were looking for. I just don't understand what anyone could possibly want from me."

"Maybe they don't want something from you. Maybe they want something from Ruby. Since you're responsible for her, maybe they think she gave something to you before she died." Nik checked the little notebook he always kept in his coat pocket. "Every place Ruby visited, or anyone's place connected to her, has been ransacked. Her trailer back in Cloudsville. Her motel room here in Clearview. Richard Baker's house. The morgue in Newcomer Funeral Home. Tammy the bookkeeper's house. And now your house, Kalli."

"It definitely seems like a pattern," I said. "Someone is retracing Kalli's steps and the people who had access to her body. The question is why. What did Ruby have that someone was willing to kill for?"

Nik locked eyes with me. "If we answer that million-dollar question, we just might find our killer."

~

"OH, MY POOR BABY," Ma said, fussing over every inch of me. *What did that monster do to you? Why, when I get my hands on--*

"Ma, please." I stepped out of her grasp. "I'm fine."

I went to work the next morning as usual, trying to maintain a low profile. I should have known the rumor mill would spread the news of my attack before sunrise. Ma and Aunt Tasoula had descended on Full Disclosure before we had even opened the doors.

"You no fine," Aunt Tasoula said. "You sound like a froggy." She came at me with a makeup brush. "Here, let me. I fix you booboo."

I jumped back. "I'm good. Really." Lord only knew where that makeup brush had been. I didn't want anyone else's dead skin cells anywhere near my flesh. I spun my fidget ring three times for good measure.

Aunt Tasoula shrugged. "Your loss." Then she proceeded to powder her nose, which is exactly what I suspected.

I loved my aunt dearly, but she had seriously been about to use her own personal make-up brush on me. After her *big plans* and stripper pole and pulled blinds so she could *tease the strip*...I didn't want anything of hers anywhere near me.

"Ladies, I have an idea," Jaz said. "I heard Boomer

talking about Mandy's Massage Parlor to Nik. I've always wanted to go there. Why don't we go treat ourselves to a spa day? That would make Kalli feel better for sure."

"I could use a good facial." Aunt Tasoula patted her cheeks.

"Maybe a bit of pampering would do my Kalli good," Ma agreed.

"Yes, it's settled then," Jaz said. "Facials for all."

I looked at Jaz like she had three heads.

She knew I hated to be touched on a good day, and even more so now that I could hear other people's thoughts. After just getting attacked, there was no way I wanted someone's hands on me again anytime soon. I was about to say something, when she grabbed both my hands with hers and gave me a warning look.

The spa isn't the only thing our boys were talking about. Grayson Millbrook followed Richard Baker there. They've been seen together a few times, and you heard Baker at your aunt's salon. He told Millbrook he was going to regret not leaving with him. He also said to remember what they talked about, and they would be square. We can't let this opportunity to find out more pass us by.

I arched an eyebrow. *We?*

Anyone who messes with my best friend, messes with me. She gave me a look. *Duh!*

"What's wrong with your faces?" Aunt Tasoula squinted at both of us. "Why you staring and straining at each other?"

"Ah, I see it," Ma said. "They look constipated." She shook her bees' nest. "You drink Aloe. That will fix you right up."

"I go get some." Aunt Tasoula headed for the door.

"No need." I let go of Jaz's hands. "I think she's right. A facial might just be exactly what I need."

Ma's eyes widened. She'd been trying to *fix* me my whole life. "I knew Detective Stevens was good for you. Let's go. I drive."

What on earth had I gotten myself into?

~

MANDY'S MASSAGE PARLOR was a high-class spa in a stand-alone brick building on the outskirts of town. I had heard a lot of people visited there, and it was pricey. That would make sense for a wealthy businessman like Grayson Millbrook, and a man who come from money like Richard Baker to frequent a place like this.

These days as many men frequented the spa as women.

Maybe the men met during the Harvest Festival and now were involved in a new business venture together? Or maybe their dealings had something to do with Ruby. Both men were rich through different means and could have been the answer to her money troubles. Grayson had been obsessed with her and single, but she refused him time and again. Yet she had an affair with Richard even though he was a married man.

Whatever they were up to, we needed answers.

"Oh, this is gonna be so fun." Aunt Tasoula led the way inside the massage parlor with a skip in her step. "Maybe I get full body massage."

"Why does that no surprise me?" Ma grunted.

Mandy's eyes widened briefly when she saw us before her face transformed back into a professional one. She stepped in front of the reception desk herself, dressed in clothes that screamed she had money as well.

"Can I help you ladies?"

"I'll have full body facial," Aunt Tasoula said, flipping her long hair over her shoulder and winked at us.

"Which one? The full body or the facial?" Mandy asked.

"Yes!" Aunt Tasoula nodded while grinning wide.

Ma sighed. "She no get enough oxygen to the brain."

"Ah," was all Mandy said.

"We're here for facials," Jaz clarified.

"Very well. I'll get your rooms ready if you want to have a seat in the waiting room behind you.

We nodded and did as she asked. I looked around the spa, but I didn't see Grayson or Richard, even though their cars were definitely in the parking lot. The place was busy with men and women. Some I recognized and others were out-of-towners.

Lois Flannigan came out of a room off to the side, looking thoroughly relaxed. She spotted me and walked over. "Oh, my dear, I heard what happened to you." She tsked. "I used to feel safe in Clearview, but I fear our town is going downhill fast. Mayor Riboldazzi is up for re-election, and I'm not so sure he'll get my vote if things don't change."

"Detective Stevens and Detective Matheson are working hard to crack this case. I'm sure our streets will be safe again in no time." I tried to sound reassuring which was difficult when my voice was so raspy.

"Tea with honey, dear." She patted my hand.

"Or aloe," Ma seconded.

Lois cocked her head to the side, her forehead puckering. She opened her mouth about to say something.

"Your skin is glowing. What did you have done today?" I changed the subject before Lois could get Ma started on the benefits of Aloe.

"Well, thank you, dear." She beamed, turning her face left then right so we could admire the results. "I had the hydration facial. It's wonderful."

"Do you come here a lot?" Jaz asked.

"Oh, no. It's way too expensive for my budget, but Elouise and Fay love to come here. I found a great coupon, so I was able to join them."

I scanned the waiting room. "Where are they?"

"I told them not to wait for me. They're getting us a table for lunch at Vincenzo's." Lois clapped her hands. "We're talking wedding plans."

"How fun," Jaz said.

"Toodles." Lois waved and headed outside.

Jaz leaned close to me and whispered, "I thought your mother would flip when Lois mentioned eating at Vinny's place."

"You have a point," I whispered back. Frowning, I looked around. "Where *is* Ma? I don't see Aunt Tasoula, either."

"Maybe they got called in, and we missed it?" Jaz headed to the reception desk, and I followed. "Excuse me, did the other ladies in our party get called yet?"

The woman checked her list. "No, they asked where the restroom was."

"Thank you." I walked away, and Jaz followed. I gave her a look she couldn't misinterpret. "You thinking what I'm thinking?"

"Those two together spells nothing but trouble." She groaned.

"Exactly. Let's go."

I led the way in the back to the restrooms. We went inside the ladies' room and searched everywhere, but the room was empty. Nothing bothered Jaz. She knocked on the door to the gentlemen's room and asked if two crazy Greek mamas had entered, earning her a few bizarre looks and definite no's.

"They wouldn't have left, would they?" Jaz asked.

"We would have seen them," I responded.

Chewing my bottom lip, I noticed an unmarked door, leading to the very back of the massage parlor. No one was around, so I tested the doorknob.

It opened.

"Where on earth does this lead?" Jaz asked.

"There's only one way to find out."

I stepped over the threshold and walked down a long hallway. There were several doors on either side of the hallway, but something kept drawing me to the last one at the end of the hall. We stopped just outside the door.

"You call me crazy? I show you crazy," I heard the unmistakable sound of Ma's voice on the other side of the door, followed by the distinct sound of a whip snapping.

"Oh, my Zeus." I grabbed the nob and turned the handle to open the door.

I gasped.

Jaz barked out a laugh.

Aunt Tasoula was wrapped only in a towel. She sat high in the air on a swing, holding a glass of amber liquid, kicking her legs and singing, "Red Rum, Red Rum, whatcha gonna do? Whatcha gonna do when I come for you." She giggled and looked at her glass. "Why you no red?"

Ma was also wrapped only in a towel. She stood there like Nike, the Greek goddess of speed, strength, and victory. She held a whip in her hand, and a man dressed in a black uniform cowered on the floor.

"Ma! What are you doing?"

"This man insult me. He say I need fifty blades."

"Fifty shades," the man mumbled.

"Fifty shaves?" Ma cracked her whip above his head again. "Shaves, schmaves. I Greek, but I no *that* hairy! Who needs fifty blades to shave?" She shook her bees' nest. "Do I look like a man? You shave my face; I shave your head." She cracked the whip again.

"Ma! Put the whip down."

"No. Not until he say sorry."

"What is happening? I'm so confused," the man said, looking pale. "I asked if they wanted the Red Room and the Fifty Shades package. That songbird up there asked for Red Rum and if she could buy this swing for her shop. Then this Amazon warrior screamed and started swinging all these toys at me."

I looked around the room in horror. It was a deep red. The walls were covered with all these scary contraptions and devices I'd never seen before and, frankly, didn't want to know anything about.

I swallowed hard. "Ma, I think it's time to go."

"Not until I get what I paid for."

"We booked facials, Ma. This room is *not* for facials. You don't need to be undressed for a facial."

"Facials can be messy. What this room for? Shaving?" She snapped her whip again. "I no hairy, I say."

"Red Rum, Red Rum, whatcha gonna do? Whatcha gonna do when I come for you?" Aunt Tasoula giggled louder and then hiccupped.

"Aunt Tasoula, get down from there. You're going to break your neck."

"Okay." She jumped down, not spilling a drop, then turned to the cowering man. "I'll take it. How much for the swing?"

The man looked at us and mouthed, *Help me.*

"I think we know why the men weren't out front," Jaz said.

"Mandy's Massage Parlor isn't just a high-class spa, is it?"

"I'm pretty sure it's a front for an erotic massage parlor in the back, with Richard Baker and Grayson Millbrook at the center of it all."

Nicole Archer

"I think we can keep the lid on until I figure out how," Sal said.

"And what are we gonna do in a high-class spa—"

The petite girl was a foot from the static masses ... motion in the black, with Luck and Buster and Carson still blind at the core of it ..."

CHAPTER 16

Later that night, Nik and I went grocery shopping at Sal's Supermarket. We spent a lot of time at each other's half of the house: eating, sleeping, hanging out. We might as well shop together. We'd gotten over our break, but still hadn't defined what we were. Complicated, is what I liked to call it. I couldn't seem to live with him, yet I definitely couldn't live without him.

Like I had a choice. He was sticking to his word and not letting me out of his sight. I touched a hand to my neck and loosened the scarf I'd donned to hide the bruises.

If I had someone else with me, he was fine with it, but if I was going somewhere alone, he insisted on coming with me. To the point where he planned his work schedule around my comings and goings. He seemed to be more nervous about my safety than I was. It was a good thing my detective was dreamy.

He was driving me crazy!

"Hi, Sal, how are you?" I asked as I stopped by his office while Nik grabbed us a shopping cart.

Sal shrugged. "I'm okay. Keeping my head down

and nose out of trouble. I have the wife and kids to think about, so it's not worth trying to prove I'm right."

"About what?" Detective Stevens pulled up beside us.

He looked cute pushing our shopping cart. Comfortable. *Normal*. It gave me hope that we could work out as an official couple. Maybe Father Conery was right. Maybe it was time I put myself out there and try.

Sal's eyes met Nik's and he cleared his throat, snapping me back to the conversation at hand. "Ruby's guilt in shoplifting at my store. My innocence in her death. I'll admit I'm a hothead. It's hard for me to hold my tongue when I know I'm right about something. But I can also admit my mouth has gotten me into trouble before, but I'm no murderer. I have a family to think about."

"Understandable."

Sal pointed up. "By the way, I did get all new security cameras that see every part of my store."

"That's great, Sal. Good for you." Nik gave him his card. "Call me if anything else comes up."

"Will do." Sal nodded once to Nik and smiled at me. "Say hello to your parents for me. Your grandmother, too. I haven't seen her in forever."

"I will."

Sal disappeared back inside his office.

Nik and I started down the aisles, checking our lists and putting items in the cart. "What do you want for dinner tonight?" I asked.

"Not Red Rum," Nik said on a scoff and shook his head. "The trouble those two get into is unbelievable."

"I know. I couldn't make this stuff up if I tried."

"All this time, and Mandy got away with running a prostitution ring out of her *massage* parlor. She was smart. Most sex trafficking or prostitution rings use

massage parlors as a front, but there are usually signs
that give them away."

"Really, like what?"

"Well, for one, their prices are often lower than the
norm. The women or men performing the services
usually ask for a large tip and are distressed if they
don't get it. They appear to be living at the business.
The hours are later than normal, and often, the front
door is locked. You can't get in unless you're buzzed in
or enter through a side or back door. Darkened front
windows. Suspicious things like that."

"Mandy definitely had a legitimate massage parlor
in front." I pondered her business. "Her prices were
higher than normal, and half the socialites like Fay
Baker and Elouise Sinclaire frequented her business."
I ran a hand over my face. "I don't really like facials,
but those women are going to be horrified when they
hear the spa that was much more than just a *spa* has
been shut down."

"They'll get over it as soon as gossip turns to something else. That's what people like them do. As for
Mandy, she doesn't run a sex trafficking operation. She
was smart enough to employ high-end prostitutes,
both male and female, who knew exactly what they
were getting into. None of them were coerced."

"You mean some people actually *want* to be a
prostitute?"

"There's good money in it for them. Whereas
human traffickers use psychological means to traffic
sex by tricking and manipulating or even threatening
their victims into providing commercial sex for
money. And the victims don't receive any of the
money."

"That's horrible."

"And far too common."

"So, what happens now?"

"It doesn't matter that the participants are willing. Prostitution is still illegal in Connecticut. Mandy is out of business and facing jail time for sure."

"All because of my red rum drinking, crazy swinging Aunt Tasoula and my insulted, whip-wielding goddess of a mama. I can't keep up with them." I rubbed my aching temples. "Like I said, I couldn't make this stuff up if I tried."

"Truth is always stranger than fiction for sure." Nik laughed.

"You wouldn't be laughing if *your* Ma was a part of these shenanigans."

That sobered him up real quick.

"No, I definitely would not." He looked at the paper in his hand. "Let's get back to shopping."

"Okay, we were talking about what we wanted for dinner tonight," I said, when we heard raised voices one aisle over. "What's that?"

Nik held up his finger in a shushing motion.

"You can't keep staying at the funeral home, Wally," Mable Griffith's voice said. "It's not healthy. You need to get out more."

"I'm here with you now, aren't I?"

"Only because I guilted you into coming with me to stock the office fridge for your poor employees. If you won't let them leave to eat their lunch at a restaurant or anywhere else, then the least you can do is provide them with office drinks and snacks. I certainly can't afford to keep buying take out for everyone."

"No one asked you to do that."

"I know." She sighed. "I was just trying to be nice. You know I have a hard time making friends. You all were so nice when I moved here five years ago. You guys are like a family to me. When you're upset, I'm upset, too."

"I know. I'm sorry. We all care about you, too. It's just I can't get over what happened. Ruby's body never should have gone missing while under my care. Ophelia Ballas was the only person who was nice to me back in high school, so I know how you feel when people care about you. I would do anything for Ophelia and her family. She doesn't deserve to be accused of murder, or for her daughter to be going through all this drama."

"You have to stop punishing yourself. You didn't do anything wrong," Mable said with a gentleness to her tone.

"That's a matter of opinion." There was a pause before he continued. "All I know is I'm going to do everything in my power to find out who took Ruby's body and recover it before it's too late. I owe Ophelia that much."

I accidentally bumped an endcap while trying to peek around the corner of the aisle. Several cans went crashing to the floor and rolling away. Detective Dreamy raised a brow at me and shook his head.

"Whoopsy daisy," I said, swinging my cart around the aisle. "Guess I'd better pay attention when driving this thing. Objects are closer than they appear in the grocery aisle and all that." I laughed.

They didn't.

I cleared my throat and bent over to pick up my mess.

"Any news on where Ruby's body is?" Wally asked Detective Dreamy. He looked even worse than the last time I saw him. He hadn't shaved and he was even thinner if that were possible.

"We have a couple leads we're following, but

nothing concrete as of yet." Nik gave him the once over. "How are you holding up?"

Wally brushed him off. "Don't worry about me."

"How's Tammy?" I asked.

"A little spooked, but that's to be expected," Wally said.

"Wally gave her time off to recover from the break-in." Mable looked up at Detective Stevens. "Too bad no one can give *him* time off."

Wally whipped his head in her direction with a frown.

Mable ignored him, looking at the detective the whole time. "He wouldn't take it anyway." She sighed.

"I'll let you know if any leads turn up." Nik handed Wally his card. "Please return the courtesy." He always handed out a card even if he'd already handed one out earlier. He didn't want to give anyone an excuse for not contacting him if they had any news.

"You can count on me, sir."

"But can the rest of us?" Mable muttered and then walked out of the grocery story, leaving Wally staring after her with a helpless expression on his face.

WE'D STAYED in and cooked dinner last night, and it was a disaster. Nik didn't like the tofu I made, and I didn't care for the fish he burned on the grill. Thank goodness for Sunday brunch at his Ma's house today.

Chloe's back yard had a big gazebo, marble statues and a fountain in the middle just like my parents' yard. These brunches would move inside soon as the temperatures grew colder. For now, it was a mild fall day, and Chloe had large heat lamps scattered around the lawn.

"It was great seeing everyone in church today," I said to Chloe.

"You and me both. I thought for sure Father would ban your mama for another two weeks once he found out about the fifty blades and the Red Rum, but he didn't say a word about any of it."

"Fighting in church is not allowed but going to church for guidance is encouraged. I think Father likes feeling needed," Nik said.

"I heard about the Red Rum and the fifty blades," Chloe said with wide eyes. "The girls asked me to go, but I couldn't, thank goodness. Quincy would not have liked me up on a swing one bit." She waggled her eyebrows. "Unless he was the one pushing it."

"Alright, alright," Nik said. "I don't need to hear that."

"Neither did Pop," I said. "Ma went to confession after she realized what type of massage she almost had. I thought Ma would end up back at Doc's for sure. Aunt Tasoula bought the swing, of course." I shook my head.

Both the Ballas and Pagonis families were there, as well as Jaz and Boomer. Nik and I walked over to join them.

"Now there's a sight I didn't think I'd see anytime soon." Jaz pointed to a group of chairs around one of the heat lamps.

I looked over and saw Jasper sitting between both Thalia and Eleni. The three were actually talking and smiling.

"Maybe they formed a truce and decided to all just be friends since Jasper isn't staying in town permanently," I said. "That would be nice. I like the guy."

"Me, too," Jaz said.

Nik and Boomer both frowned at us, and we rolled our eyes on a laugh.

Father Papadopoulos walked in with Father Conery and Sister Mary Margaret. They looked around, and then they all stopped over to talk to Chloe, Captain Crenshaw, and my parents.

"What do you think that's about?" I asked.

"I'm not sure, but I'm going to find out." Nik looked at Boomer. "You coming, Matheson?"

"I wouldn't miss it." Boomer walked away with Nik; their heads bent together deep in discussion.

"Father Papadopoulos stopping by isn't unusual," I said, "but it does seem a little strange to see Father Conery and Sister Mary Margaret here."

"Boomer and I aren't Greek, and we're welcome," Jaz said.

"You guys are like family. Not that they wouldn't be welcome either, it's just we barely know them, and Sunday brunch is usually reserved just for family. It makes me think this might be about more than a social visit."

"Well, we'll find out soon enough. The guys are coming back this way."

Neither of us said a word until they reached our sides.

"You look so serious," I said to Nik.

"So do you," Jaz said to Boomer.

"Salvatore Stallone was attacked leaving the catholic church this morning," Boomer replied gravely.

Nik made eye contact with me. "He was strangled...only he didn't make it."

My heart bottomed out. "He's dead?"

"I'm afraid so." Nik rubbed the back of his neck, looking tense.

"Oh, no, his poor family," Jaz said.

"It looks like his attacker is the same person who nearly killed Kalli."

I gasped.

"That's not all," Boomer added.

"What more could there possibly be?" Jaz asked.

"He left something in the confessional."

"Like what?" I asked, barely able to speak. My mind couldn't comprehend this horrible turn of events.

"A thumb drive," Nik replied, looking at his notes. "I think we now know what our killer has been looking for."

"Sal told Captain Crenshaw that he found the thumb drive hidden in the Health and Beauty Aisle. Sal thinks Ruby hid it there and then shop lifted in hopes he would find it and bring it to the police. Sal either accidentally forgot it in the confessional, or he meant for Father Conery to find it. Whatever the reason, Captain Crenshaw has it now."

"What's on it?" I asked.

"That's another million-dollar question we're about to find the answer to."

CHAPTER 17

"I no believe I doing this." Ma held a tray of Mosaiko as we stood in front of the doors to Vincenzo's Restaurant.

"We're not here for Vinny, Ma. We're here to pay our respects to Angelina," I said from beside her. "Salvatore Stallone was Italian, and Vincenzo's was his favorite restaurant. You must accept that."

She thrust her chin up high. "Ah, but he loved my dessert best."

"Yes, he did." I patted her arm.

She nodded once, and then marched through the front door and didn't stop until she reached the bar. She set her tray down in the middle of all the other food, as the centerpiece. "This no for him." She thrust her finger at Vincenzo Ricci. "This for her." She swept her hand toward Angelina Stallone in a grand gesture.

"Why, I ought to—" Vinny started.

"Oh, woe is me, you poor thing." Ma hugged Angelina hard and didn't let go. "I here for you now. Everything will be okay. You'll see." She glared at Vinny over the crying woman's shoulder.

Vinny threw his hands up and marched down to

the end of the bar. I did a double take. Danny Ferrari sat there, his dark eyes drilling into me. All I could do was stare back as a chill infused my every cell. I still got such bad vibes from him. My eyes dropped lower, and I sucked in a breath.

His hand had an ace bandage on it.

All I could think was he'd bruised it while strangling me and then killing poor Sal. I lifted my gaze back to his face, but he was already in deep conversation with Vinny. Maybe they really were plotting a way to get back at Ma. Vinny could have hired a thug to do his dirty work for him.

Going after Ophelia Ballas's only child would destroy her for sure.

"I still can't believe he's gone." Angelina drew my attention back to the conversation at hand. "And in such a horrible way. To be strangled right after leaving church is unthinkable. Who does that?"

"Satan." Ma made the sign of the cross. "Evil no win against good. They will be brought to justice. I know this to be true. You'll see."

"I hope so." Angelina sniffled. "It's so unfair."

"I'm so sorry for your loss, Mrs. Stallone," I said, giving her a hug. I'd worn a scarf to hide my bruised neck, not wanting to remind her that I'd survived the same person who had attacked her husband when he hadn't been so lucky.

She nodded but didn't speak. *If only that woman had stayed away, none of this would have happened.*

I patted her back then stepped away, feeling the weight of guilt press down on me. Angelina was right. If Ruby hadn't come to Clearview, her husband would still be alive. I couldn't help but blame myself. If I hadn't been on the news over past murders and then the recent success of my clothing line, then Ruby wouldn't have come to town.

Why did I have to look so much like her?

"What's wrong, kopelia mou?" Ma wiped a tear from my face. She'd always called me *my girl* since I was little, mostly when she knew I was hurting.

Others had come into the restaurant to pay their respects to Angelina, so she'd moved down the row of people to great them. It was just Ma and me standing in our spot by the bar now. I hadn't even realized I'd been crying.

"Nothing."

"It's not nothing. I know you. You are blaming yourself. Just because you look like your birth mother, does *not* mean you are like her. You are my girl." She patted her chest. "Like me. You no forget that." She hugged me hard, and for once didn't have any thoughts. Just waves of love pouring out of her. She kissed my cheek before stepping back. "Now wipe those tears and show them what a strong, fine Ballas woman you are."

"I love you so much, Ma," I said and meant it with every fiber of my being.

Her face melted. "I love you, too, Kalliope. More than you'll ever know." She wiped her cheek. "Now you make *me* cry."

Wally greeted Angelina a few feet away from us and told her that when Mable released Sal's body, he would drop everything to discuss the funeral arrangements. Angelina thanked him and then he started to walk away.

"Wallace Newcomer, you gonna leave without saying hello?" Ma hollered and wore a mock stern look on her face.

Wally whipped his head around in surprise, then

gave her a sheepish grin and walked over to us. "Sorry, Ophelia, I didn't see you there."

I could tell by the look on his face and the slump to his shoulders that he felt the same guilt that I did. I blamed myself for Ruby coming to town, and he blamed himself for allowing Ruby to vanish.

Ma patted her beehive and stood a little straighter, her hair swaying left and right as she wiggled her head. "I'm hardly unforgettable." She winked.

His lips tipped up slightly with fondness. "No, you are definitely not, Ophelia. You're one of a kind. Though I am surprised to see you here of all places."

"Bah, I no here for Vinny. I here for Angelina." She poked him in the ribs and frowned. "You too skinny. You come to a real restaurant. I'll fatten you up."

He rubbed his rib and chuckled. "I just might do that. Now, I really have to go. So much work to do these days unfortunately." He waved by to us and then walked through the restaurant and out the door.

I glanced at the end of the bar, but Danny was gone.

"I should get going, too, Ma. I have an early day at work tomorrow."

"Okay, but first, I need a favor from you."

"Just say the word."

She raised a brow. "I trying to, but you no listen."

I zipped my lips together and pretended to throw away the key.

"My bunions are killing me after teasing the strip, and I think I pulled my shoulder when whipping the crack."

My eyes sprang wide. "You mean cracking the whip."

"That's what I say. See? You no listen."

Yup. I was keeping my mouth shut over that one.

"You meet me at Aphrodite's, and I give you Mosaiko to take to the Clearview Motel," she went on. "It's no for Gary this time. It's for Angelina's out of town family, okay? Okay. You good girl." She pulled out her cell phone.

"Hop in. I'll give you a ride."

"I no hop in matchbox car. I call your papa and meet you there."

We had met at Vincenzo's Restaurant because Pop had dropped her off. Someone had to run the restaurant, and Ma had insisted on representing the family. She'd asked me to go, so I'd said yes. It made no sense not to ride together now, but Ma didn't make sense most of the time. I don't know why I thought tonight might be any different.

~

THE DAYS WERE GROWING SHORTER and darker. A light rain started to fall, whipping up a flurry of colorful leaves. I drove slowly through town and headed toward the Clearview Motel with the dessert Ma had given me for Stallone relatives who had come in from out of town.

Nik would not be happy with me right now.

Ma had been with me when paying our respects to the Stallone family at Vinny's, but after I picked up the dessert from Aphrodite's, she'd stayed behind to help Pop. I couldn't blame her. The restaurant was slammed. But for me to go out to the Clearview Motel alone at night would scare Nik to death.

I was an adult and didn't need anyone's permission to do things on my own, but I knew my Dreamy Detective was just worried about me since I'd nearly been strangled to death. I admitted I was worried myself. Salvatore Stallone had been one of our own. For him to be murdered by the same person who had tried to murder me hit too close to home.

In my defense, I'd tried to call Nik, but he had been with Detective Matthews all day, going over the thumb drive, and didn't call me back. I was just dropping off dessert. What harm could come from that?

The motel was on the outskirts of town, so I had to take back roads to get there. The streets were pretty deserted with the rain growing heavier. I noticed a pair of headlights behind me, so I slowed down to let them pass.

They didn't.

I made a turn, and they did the same. I made another, and so did they. I sped up, and they stayed right on my bumper. By the time I reached the motel driveway, I took the turn on two wheels, spraying a puddle of water on a couple entering the motel. They jumped back, and I mouthed *sorry* as I pulled into a spot right up front.

The car pulled into a spot directly behind me.

Grabbing my tray of Mosaiko, I got out of the car not sure which was more terrifying. The person following me or Ma if she found out I'd smushed her dessert. I turned around to face who was behind me, refusing to allow anyone to surprise me from behind again.

Danny Ferrari stood there, staring at me with his usual intensity.

"Why are you following me?" I took a step back.

"I'm not. I'm staying at the motel. Why are *you* stalking me?" He took a step forward.

I took another step back. "Why are you wearing gloves?"

He frowned. "Because it's cold out."

We were the only ones in the parking lot now, and the rain was falling harder. I kept the soggy, smushed Mosaiko between us. "They're black," I pointed out.

"I like black." He took another step forward.

I stood my ground with my tray ready to be a weapon. "How'd you hurt your hand?"

His eyes widened. "How'd you know I hurt my hand?"

"I saw the bandage earlier at Vincenzo's."

"Why so many questions?" He narrowed his eyes.

"Why won't you answer?" I paused a beat to let my words sink in. "Is it because you sprained your hand strangling me and killing Salvatore Stallone?"

He gaped at me. "You think I killed Sal?" He ran a hand over his dark buzz cut, his even darker eyes looking confused. "I can't do this anymore." He sighed. "You know me." His gaze drilled into mine. "I'm not a murderer. I'm—"

The front door of the motel opened, and Grayson Millbrook ran out, dragging his luggage with him. He stopped and stared at us for a moment, then bolted toward his car. Sirens wailed and flew into the parking lot, blocking the entrance.

Detective Mathews and Detective Stone got out of their vehicles and drew their weapons. Grayson dropped his luggage, stood up straight, and raised his hands in the air.

"Grayson Millbrook, you're under arrest," Nik said, handcuffing the man. "You have the right to remain silent and refuse to answer questions. Anything you say may be used against you in a court of law. You have the right to an attorney before speaking with the police and to have an attorney present during questioning now and in the future. If you cannot afford an attorney, one will be appointed for you before questioning if you wish. If you decide to answer questions now without an attorney present, you have the right to stop at any time until you talk to an attorney. Do you understand these rights and willing to answer our questions without an attorney present?"

"I have a whole team of attorneys, Detective," Grayson said smugly. "You're going to be sorry you arrested me."

"Are you threatening a police officer?" Boomer asked.

"Just informing you of the facts. What exactly am I being arrested for?"

"I'm pretty sure you know, given your attempt at a hasty getaway," Boomer said with a snort.

"I've concluded my business, and Ruby's body is still missing. There's no longer a reason for me to stay."

"You're being arrested for being a part of a three-county-wide prostitution ring," Nik said, his style professional and to the point, void of emotion.

"You never loved Ruby," Boomer growled, his style full of emotion. "Your ego couldn't handle that she shot you down. She knew you were involved in things that scared her more than being addicted to drugs. She might have been a stripper, but she wasn't a prostitute."

The men might be vastly different in their approach, but they were both great detectives and they worked well together.

"You have no proof of any of this." Grayson oozed confidence.

"On the contrary," Nik said. "Ruby was no fool. She knew if you didn't get what you wanted from her, you might harm her. So, she gathered the proof she needed to ruin you. She blackmailed you with her proof to keep you away."

"Then why would I follow her to Clearview if that were the case?" Grayson looked down his nose at the detectives. "You gentlemen are grasping at anyone to pin Ruby's murder on. It won't work, and you'll look like a fool for coming after someone of my caliber."

"I'm pretty sure we'll be seen as heroes for going after a scumbag like you," Boomer ground out.

"You followed Ruby because you couldn't risk there being proof of your shady dealings out there," Nik continued logically. "When you couldn't find the proof, you killed her. Then you continued to look for the proof by breaking into all the places she had been and the people who had contact with her."

"There is no proof," Grayson said, looking bored.

"Correction. You didn't find any proof." Nik held up the thumb drive. "This is what you were looking for."

Grayson's face paled. "I've never seen that before."

"That doesn't mean your name isn't on it."

"Admit it," Boomer said. "You killed Salvatore Stallone because you heard he found something in his store that Ruby left behind. You just didn't realize he left it in the confessional for Father Conery."

"You're both crazy. I don't need to buy a woman's affection."

"Mandy's Massage Parlor is a front for an erotic massage prostitution ring. Pearl found the prostitutes and Mandy provided the place. You provided the clientele."

"I've never been to Mandy's Massage Parlor."

"Yes, he has. I saw his car parked in the back," I blurted, drawing surprised eyes in my direction. I'd been standing there like a statue the whole time, but no one had noticed in all the chaos. "Cake anyone?" I laughed nervously.

No one was amused.

"Look, I'm not admitting to anything," Grayson said. "But even if I was involved, there's no way I could have pulled all of that off on my own."

"Richard Baker has already been arrested and ratted you out, so you might as well confess," Boomer said.

"I have alibis during a lot of those break-ins, and Richard's house was broken into as well. How do you explain that?"

"You took turns breaking in to give the other an alibi," Nik said. "And breaking into Richard's house made for a great cover story. You provided wealthy businessmen, while Richard knew plenty of rich philanthropists."

"You guys think you're so smart, but you're not." Grayson smirked. "There's a name not on that list. A person with more power than any of us and connections that go far beyond three counties, businessmen, and philanthropists."

"Yeah, right." Boomer snorted. "You expect us to believe you?"

"I expect my lawyers will use it as a bargaining chip. I'm through talking, Detectives. Let's get this over with so I can post bail."

Boomer helped Grayson into the squad car and shut the door in his face. "Do you believe him?"

Nik creased his brow. "My instincts tell me he's telling the truth."

"Mine, too." Boomer scowled. "What are we going to do?"

"Figure out that last name at any cost."

"Roger that." Boomer nodded. "Meet you at the station?"

"In a minute." Nik's hard gaze found mine. "I need to see a lady about a cake."

I swallowed dryly; my appetite suddenly gone.

CHAPTER 18

"I can't believe Richard was involved in a prostitution ring." Fay Baker sobbed in the middle of the clothing racks in Full Disclosure. "Not just involved but actually helping to run the ring. That's worse than a divorce would have been."

"It doesn't surprise me that Grayson Millbrook was involved," Elouise Sinclaire responded, her burgundy hair slicked back behind her ears. Her sharp gray eyes took in every detail as she browsed the clothing racks. "That's why I don't get serious with men. He was good for a night, but that's all."

"I had to drive two hours to get my hair fixed from that crazy lady who tried to ruin me only to be ruined by my own husband." Fay touched her tight, curly blond bobbed hair.

Jaz's gaze met mine, and I just shrugged. My aunt *was* a little crazy, but in her defense, she had been standing up for Ma and me.

Lois Flannigan had suggested Elouise and Fay accompany her while shopping to take Fay's mind off her troubles. They'd started at Vixen and ended up here for the weekly sale, and to take full advantage of

Lois's coupons. Lois was thrilled to be included by such sophisticated socialites when it was clear to everyone else that they were just using her for her knowledge of all the gossip and anything going on in Clearview.

"Oh, dear, you poor thing. That man is not worthy of you." Lois's chubby rosy cheeks matched her hair. "I heard they found drugs in Grayson's possession. He obviously never saw that commercial about your brain on drugs. That's enough to scare anyone clean." Lois shuddered. "I wonder if he was Ruby's drug dealer?"

"Grayson Millbrook is a wannabe big shot." Elouise rolled her eyes. "Trust me, I'm not jealous, but that's just another reason I don't get serious with men. He made the rounds from one woman to the next to stroke his ego. He deserves what's coming to him."

"Richard used to try to get me to do drugs with him. I hate drugs. They're so beneath me." Fay's face registered her disgust, then she paused a moment. "I just realized now I can't have the party of the year." She started wailing all over again.

Elouise's face pinched in displeasure. "Snap out of it, woman. You don't need a man to have a party."

Fay blinked a little startled. "That's true." She dried her tears. "By not divorcing Richard and standing by his side while he's in prison, I'll look noble and be even more popular." She nodded, her eyes brightening. "This could be a good thing."

I looked at Jaz and raised a brow. The woman was delusional.

Lois frowned.

"Hey, maybe someone will off him in prison," Elouise said casually while moving on to another clothing rack. "Widows are all the rage."

Fay lowered her voice, "You never know what can

happen. Prison's a dangerous place." She sounded almost giddy, her eyes looking a little crazed.

Elouise laughed.

The rose left Lois's cheeks.

"Excuse me, ladies, my stomach has soured. I'm
going home to my *wonderful* husband." She turned
around and left the store without a single look back.

I mentally applauded.

"Can I help you ladies?" Jaz asked.

Elouise looked over my Kalli Original display with
a critical eye. "These aren't so original. I've seen better." Her gaze shot to me.

I shrugged, having come up against snootier
women than Elouise Sinclaire.

"Well, it wouldn't look good on you anyway," Jaz
said.

Elouise looked at her, somewhat impressed, but
then her expression changed to bored once more.

"That was rude," Fay said.

"No, that was true," Jaz replied. "This is rude. Your
hair looks terrible." She looked over the woman's tight
blond bobbed length curls. "You look like a poodle on
a bad day. I would know. I have two, but Chanel and
Versace are much classier than either of you."

"Why, I never."

"That's apparent."

"What's terrible are your clothes. They're trashy
just like her mother," Fay spat. "I wouldn't wear a
single item."

"Come on, Fay. Let's go to Cloudsville. The shopping's much better, and I need to get my nails done.
Mine are a mess." They turned around and left,
talking and laughing with their noses stuck high in
the air.

I hoped it rained.

"Women like that make me so angry," Jaz said. She was and always would be my best friend. I loved her for defending me.

"I don't let them bother me. My designs are not for everyone, but they do well with the clientele they're meant for."

"You're a better woman than I am. She called my clothes trashy."

"Your clothes aren't trashy. They're trendy." I looked out the window as the women marched down the street. "The only trash around here just walked out the door."

"HAVE YOU FORGIVEN ME YET?" I asked as Nik and I sat at his kitchen table, drinking wine and beer and having dinner.

He moaned around a mouthful of food, his eyes rolling back in pleasure.

I smiled and sipped my wine, savoring much smaller bites.

Last night, Nik had insisted on following me home. He didn't want to talk about why I was at the motel alone that time of night. He just asked me to promise him I wouldn't go anywhere else. Then he went back to the station to join Boomer in interrogating Grayson Millbrook and Richard Baker.

I was a grown woman and didn't need a babysitter, but Danny had spooked me. I was scared and didn't want to go out alone, so I chose to stay home. I knew Nik was trying hard to solve this murder case and didn't need to worry about me. I appreciated everything he was doing for our family and wanted to make it up to him by cooking one of his favorite meals.

Lamb Kleftiko.

I'd ordered all of the ingredients online and had them delivered. Then I marinated the lamb in olive oil, garlic, and lemon juice overnight. I got out of work early today and let myself into his half of the house to surprise him with this traditional Greek dish.

Besides, I owed Wolfgang lots of pets and one kiss.

After scrubbing my hands thoroughly, I had prepared the rest of the dish by adding dry white wine, potatoes, roasted peppers, and tomatoes. I'd wrapped the entire thing in parchment paper to seal in the juices and flavors, then baked it on the oven for two and a half hours. Finally, I'd paired the dish with a Greek feta salad, bean soup, and homemade pita bread.

Nik finished eating and then wiped his mouth, sitting back in his seat and looking stuffed. "Thank you for dinner. It was delicious. My YiaYia used to tell me the Klefts used to steal the lamb and cook it in the ground, both to seal in the flavors but also to hide their thievery. Even back then I was fascinated with crimes and the law."

"Very interesting, but you still didn't answer my question." I bit my bottom lip. "Have you forgiven me yet?"

He sighed. "There's nothing to forgive you for, Kalli. You didn't do anything wrong. I'm just worried sick about you. After Sal was murdered by the same person who tried to murder you, I realized I could have lost you for good." His eyes filled with moisture, and he didn't even try to hide it. "I care about you more than you know. I don't know what I would do if anything bad happened to you. I can't imagine living in a world without you in it."

My heart squeezed tight with emotion. I leaned

across the table and kissed him softly on the lips, then sat back down and wiped my own eyes. "I care about you more than you know, also. I don't want to live without you, either. I did call you first, but you didn't answer."

"I know, I saw that. I appreciate the effort." He finished his beer.

I took another sip of my wine. "So, how did the interrogation go?"

"Grayson and Baker admitted to the prostitution ring and the break-ins and using drugs, but they both deny being Ruby's drug dealer or killing her."

"Did they admit to strangling me and killing Sal?" I held my breath, hoping this nightmare might finally be over.

Nik was already shaking his head. "No, I'm sorry, Ballas."

I closed my eyes and nodded, then looked at him. "It's okay, Detective. I was afraid you were going to say that. So, my attacker is still out there and could strike again at any moment. If the attacker isn't the person doing the break-ins, then what do they want from me?"

"I'm not sure, just keep your guard up."

"What will happen to Baker and Grayson now?"

"Well, they confessed so they will definitely do jail time, but there's a catch."

"A catch? Like what?"

Nik was about to say something when his cell phone rang. "It's Detective Matheson." Nik had taken the early shift, and Boomer had the evening shift. "What's up, Boomer?" Nik listened for a minute. "Are you sure?" Nik listened again, and his face hardened. "I'll be right there."

"What's wrong?"

"Grayson and Baker will get a lesser sentence for turning in the head of the prostitution ring. Someone with a far greater reach and more powerful clients than businessmen and philanthropists."

"The catch I take it?"

Nik nodded, a muscle in his jaw bulging.

"Who is it?"

His gaze met mine and locked. "Mayor Riboldazzi."

~

"I HAVE ALL-NATURAL ICE CREAM, no sugar added." Jaz grinned wide, holding up her treasure, as I opened the door later that night.

After Nik left, I didn't want to be alone. So, I cleaned up his kitchen and got Wolfgang settled for the night, then headed home and called Jaz. I could always count on her to come to me whenever I needed her for anything. And she knew I would gladly do the same.

"What would I do without you?" I took the ice cream from her and headed to the kitchen, setting the container on the table.

"Nothing because that's never going to happen." She followed me and grabbed the bowls.

We took a moment and ate in silence, savoring the delicious treat. I mean, who doesn't like ice cream? I finished first and Prissy hopped up on my lap. Like Jaz, she seemed to know when I needed her. My gift didn't work on animals, thank goodness, because I wasn't sure I wanted to know what Prissy was thinking sometimes.

Right on cue, she hopped off my lap and walked regally out of the room with her nose in the air.

"I can't believe Mayor Riboldazzi is the head of the prostitution ring," Jaz said. "Boomer filled me in, too."

"I know. Nik was disgusted. He and Boomer and the captain work so hard to keep Clearview safe and respectable and great, and then our very own mayor goes and disgraces our town. People are going to be mortified come tomorrow when the rumor mill spreads the news." I shook my head. "And to think he was up for re-election."

"Who do you think will run?"

"I'm not sure. What do you think?"

Jaz looked pensive. "Maybe Chloe will run. She always talks about politics."

"She's dating Captain Crenshaw. I'm pretty sure that would be a conflict of interest. Besides, I'm pretty sure Nik wouldn't want his Ma as his boss."

"True. I hadn't thought of that."

"Hopefully, we'll get someone decent. We need that right now."

"Did you tell Nik about Danny?" Jaz sat back, rubbing her full stomach.

"No. I was going to, but then Boomer called, and Nik left."

"Do you think Danny could be your attacker?" Her eyes were full of concern. I could relate because I felt the same way.

"I don't know. I mean, he always looks at me in such an intense way. And his hand was injured. It takes a lot to strangle a person, let alone two, and to actually strangle someone to death. He could have easily bruised or sprained his hand."

"Did you ask him about it?"

"Yes, but he changed the subject." I folded my feet beneath me and crossed my arms over my stomach, feeling vulnerable. "He also said the strangest thing to me."

"What's that?"

"He said I knew him."

Jaz's eyebrows shot sky high.

"But then Grayson ran out and the police came, and Danny disappeared." I squinted, rubbing my temples. This whole ordeal was giving me migraines.

"Well, do you think you know him?"

"I've never heard of Danny Ferrari before, and I highly doubt I could forget those black eyes, buzz cut, and tattoos."

"What a strange comment, though."

"I know, right?" I blew out a breath of air.

"What are you going to do?" She eyed me suspiciously.

"The only thing I can." I held up my hands. "Get to the bottom of just who Danny Ferrari really is."

CHAPTER 19

"What are we doing here again?" Jaz asked as we sat in my Prius in the parking lot of the Clearview Motel early the next morning.

"We're tailing Danny," I responded.

I took a sip of my black tea as I sat crouched down in my seat and motioned for her to get lower. It was way too early for me to eat, but I'd learned my lesson the hard way last time. Pick up coffee and cinnamon buns from Maria's Sinfully Delicious Bakery before we went on a stakeout.

Hangry Jaz was scary.

"I mean we as in me. Why do I have to be with you?"

"Because I don't want to worry Nik anymore."

"Since when do you listen to him?"

"Since last night. You should have seen him at dinner." I smiled tenderly. "He was so sweet. He got all emotional talking about how much I mean to him, and he didn't know what he would do if he lost me. I've been through a lot, and I'm afraid too, but I care about him so much. I don't want to cause him any more stress or make him distracted on the job. I seriously don't know what I would do if anything bad happened to him."

"Oh, my Lord, you're in love."

"What?" I gaped at her, my heart squeezing tight. I felt like I was starting to hyperventilate. "No, I'm not." *Was I?*

"When you put someone else first and care more about their happiness than your own, that's love. That's how I knew I loved Boomer."

"B-But we're not even an official couple yet." My head was spinning with the bomb she'd just dropped on me.

"Oh, please. You shop together, eat together, sleep together...whatever that entails." She shrugged. "You're about as official as they come without the title."

I didn't kiss and tell, but let's just say my gift made a lot of things possible with Nik. I frowned. "What if my gift goes away and I can't handle being with him, or he finds out about my gift and he can't handle being with me? If I don't have him, then I can't lose him. If I let him in, I'll never be the same if we don't work out."

"I lost a year with Boomer that I'll never get back. All because I was afraid that I would hurt him, or he would hurt me. If I hadn't taken a chance, I would be lonely and miserable right now. You can't let fear and what ifs stop you from living, Kalli."

"You sound like Father Conery."

Her eyes sprang wide. "You went to see a catholic priest instead of your Greek orthodox Father Papadopoulos? Your mama's not gonna like that."

"My mama will never know." I laughed.

"How come you went to see him?"

"I wanted to talk to him about Grayson and Danny. While I was there, he asked about me. Like he really cared about how I was doing. I realized he's an impartial outsider who can be truly objective." My gaze shot to hers. "I told him about my gift."

"You did? Wow, that's a big step. What did he have to say?"

I searched my brain for his words of wisdom. "The Lord works in mysterious ways. He obviously gave me this ability for a reason. It's what I choose to do with it that's important. And he said not to squander it, but to use it for good. That's what I'm trying to do with these murder cases."

"See, he didn't think you were a freak. Neither will Nik if you just give him a chance and trust him with the truth."

"Father said life is short and precious, and I shouldn't live with regrets. He said what do I have to lose if I try? Nothing. If it doesn't work with Nik, then it doesn't work, and at least I will know. But if I never try, I will lose for sure. I might miss out on something wonderful and not to let fear of the unknown hold me back."

"He makes some good points. You should listen to him."

"He also said I should tell my detective the truth." My stomach trembled over just the thought of that conversation. "That nothing good comes from a lie. If Nik can accept me with quirks, gifts, and all, then I'll know I have something special."

"I like this dude. Maybe I should go see him."

"And risk being struck by lightning?" I teased.

"Very funny." Jaz pointed. "Hey, look. Danny's leaving."

"Buckle up because so are we."

I put the car in drive and followed at a safe distance. For the next couple of hours, we tailed Danny Ferrari. He dropped off a package at the post office, then picked up a package from Sully at the bakery, then had coffee with...

"What on earth is Danny doing having coffee with Thalia?" Jaz blurted.

My eyes narrowed, and my stomach turned over in knots. "I have no clue, but you can be sure I intend to find out." I didn't want to see her get her heart broken or feelings hurt like they did with Jasper.

Danny left the bakery and picked up what looked like white shirts beneath plastic on hangers. He stopped into Tate Hemsworth's hardware store, and then finally ended up at Vincenzo's for lunch.

"I can't see inside there." I wondered who he was meeting for lunch. "And I certainly can't go in there. Everyone knows Ma would have a fit if I stepped foot inside Vinny's restaurant. It would look suspicious."

"True, but no one will think anything if I go inside."

"Yeah, but by yourself?"

"I will say I'm meeting a friend, then I'll look around. After a few minutes, I'll say my friend can't make it after all, and I'll leave. Easy peasy."

"Nothing is ever easy peasy with you, my friend." I chewed my bottom lip. "But I can't think of anything else to do, so have at it. I'll stay parked in the back of the parking lot and keep watch."

Jaz bounced out of the car, much peppier in the afternoon with coffee and sugar in her system than she was in the morning. Several minutes went by. Father Conery and Sister Mary Margaret showed up, and I ducked lower when they parked near my car. I slowly sat up after they headed inside.

Moments later, Jaz came out skipping faster than Frona back to my car. She loved gossip and was bursting at the seams with her news.

"Hurry up and get in here," I said as I opened the window.

She hopped inside and shut the door, then I rolled the window back up. She just sat there grinning at me, loving the buildup of anticipation. She should have been a member of the Ballas family with all the drama.

Ready, set, go...Act III.

"Well?" I blurted. "You're killing me."

"Danny Ferrari and Elouise Sinclaire are sitting in a dark corner, looking pretty cozy to me."

"Wow, that woman sure does get around."

"No kidding." Jaz snorted out a laugh. "Oh, and I saw Father Conery and that nun eating lunch. I smiled and he waved and smiled back. I don't think lightning would strike me in *his* church."

I laughed. "It was just a figure of speech, Jaz."

"I know, but I still might go see him. I could use a good impartial listener to dump my troubles onto. It's cheaper than therapy, right?"

"That's one way of looking at it."

"Duck. Here comes Danny and Elouise." I slid down in my seat so just my eyes could see over the dash, and Jaz did the same. We'd been sitting there for an entire meal.

"Why aren't they leaving?" Jaz asked a few minutes later.

I frowned. "I don't know, but that doesn't look very cozy to me."

Danny and Elouise were standing in the parking lot, arguing about something. Danny's injured hand flailed about as he let loose a string of words in Italian.

Elouise backed up a step, but held her ground, and shouted right back. I didn't like the woman, but I wasn't about to let Danny hurt anyone else.

I knew what I had to do.

~

"I'VE SEEN you talking with Grayson and Richard," Elouise said, her voice laced with accusations.

"I've talked to a lot of people in this town," Danny replied, clearly frustrated. "That doesn't mean I know them or am friends with them."

"But you do business in town. I've seen you getting packages. Were you supplying them with drugs before they got arrested? Did you know Ruby Winehouse?" She kept rapid firing questions at him.

"I don't do drugs, and I did not know this Ruby person. I am in town for other reasons, which I'm beginning to regret. Now you need to back off, lady. I'm done with you." He started to walk away, but she grabbed his wounded hand. He howled and shrugged her off, and she fell to the ground.

That was all I needed to see.

I went running from my hiding spot behind their cars. "Leave her alone, you animal," I shouted, holding my hands in a ready position like I'd been taught. I needed to practice my self-defense more often. It was true. If you don't use it, you lose it. I could only hope my muscle memory would kick in and help me remember the movements.

"She's the animal. I was only defending myself." He held his wounded hand, and his face looked as if he were in pain.

I pointed to a cowering Elouise. "Yet she's the one on the ground."

Elouise let out a whimper.

"I'm beginning to think coming to this town was a mistake. I should have chosen someplace else." Danny started backing slowly away toward his car. "You're all nuts. The whole lot of you."

"And you're not going anywhere," Jaz said, pulling out her phone. "I'm calling the police."

"Please do," he said.

She arched a brow but continued to dial.

I reached down and pulled Elouise to her feet. *I was this close to getting what I deserve, and you had to stick your nose in and ruin things again. I should have finished you off while I had the chance.*

I gasped and let go of her hand. "It was you."

Her eyes widened in shock. "H-How did you know?" she whispered, sounding stunned as she backed up a step.

"You're the one who attacked me and killed Salvatore Stallone." I stared at her in horror. How could I have missed the signs? "You're the animal, and you're going to be caged. *That's* what you deserve."

The rage I'd felt when she strangled me came bubbling back to the surface. She let out a scream, looking insane, and lunged at me. She tried to wrap her hands around my neck again, but this time I managed to block her moves. I could hear sirens off in the distance, and people shouting, but I remained laser focused on defending myself.

She would not win this time.

I ducked a blow she threw my way and managed to go on the offensive and land a blow of my own to her midsection. *That was for you, Sal.* She came at me again, when suddenly, from out of nowhere, Sister Mary Margaret dove onto Elouise, pushing her to the ground and hog tying her with lightning speed like something you'd see at a rodeo.

"Elouise Sinclaire, you're under arrest for selling drugs, and for assault and murder," Sister said in a voice that sounded anything but holy.

"Who are you?" Elouise asked as the nun pulled her to her feet.

"Special Agent Catherine O'Hara," the sister said. "We've been looking for you for a long time, Ms. Sinclaire." She informed Elouise of her Miranda Rights and stowed her in the undercover car she and Father Conery had arrived in.

Sister Mary Margaret's catlike reflexes and high-strung behavior suddenly made sense. But if she was really an undercover narcotics agent for the FBI...then who on earth was Father Conery? My gaze shifted to him as he stood beside me.

"To answer the question I see in your eyes, yes, I am a real priest." He smiled at me with kindness and spoke with sincerity. "But I used to be a criminal. I was addicted to drugs, but I cleaned up my act and became a priest. It saved my life. I give back to the community as a form of penance by working with the FBI as an informant. We've been looking for Ruby Winehouse's drug dealer for a long time. Elouise Sinclair isn't just a drug dealer. She's the kingpin across several counties."

"How did you know all of that?" My head was swirling.

"Salvatore Stallone found the thumb drive which exposed the prostitution ring, but that wasn't all. There was a note from Ruby. It said she was afraid she was going to die soon. She left the thumb drive as evidence Grayson was after her, and then she left the note as evidence that Elouise Sinclair was her drug dealer. Ruby couldn't afford to pay her dealer, but this wasn't just any dealer. This was a kingpin, and Ruby knew Elouise wouldn't stop until she got her money. So, I gave the thumb drive to the police and the note to the FBI."

"I-I used my gift for good," was all I could think to say. My head was pounding, and my body felt like it was going into shock.

"I see that, my child. You did great." He pulled out a bottle of hand sanitizer and scrubbed his hands, his green eyes full of pride and affection.

I sucked in a breath. "It can't be."

He just stared at me with compassion and understanding.

"Are you...?"

"Yes, Kalli Ballas. I am your father, Michael Conery."

And just like Ma, the world went black around me.

CHAPTER 20

I sat in the police station, still feeling shell shocked. I had just given my statement to the police, and they were discussing something in another room.

While I was passed out, Nik and Boomer had arrived. Federal Agent Cat O'Hara filled them in on Elouise's arrest and the note from Sal that nobody else knew about, while Father Conery told them about his past and connection to me and Ruby. Boomer took Danny in for questioning, Jaz drove my car home, and Nik rode with me in the ambulance.

I woke up to smelling salts on the way to Clearview Hospital. I didn't feel I needed a hospital, but Nik insisted. He didn't say anything to me about meeting my father, but he kept watching me closely with concern. Doc LaLone said I was fine, other than a little bump on the head and being in shock.

That was to be expected, given the man I'd confided in turned out to be Dear Old Dad.

Now that I thought about it, I'd never seen him shake anyone's hands. His were always folded in front of him—a trick I used to keep people from trying to shake my hand. I didn't look a thing like him, but I definitely had his quirks and a few of his mannerisms.

When I'd thought of my biological father, I had imagined him to be a low-life drug dealer still. I never dreamed he would be a priest now. He'd changed so much, based on what I knew of him. He was a kind and compassionate and caring man.

His words from our conversation came back to me....

"Your mother couldn't have been too horrible. She chose to give you life and give you up to a family she knew could do far better for you than she could. It's been a long time since your birth. She's most likely had a tough time of things."

"Life can change a person for the good or bad. If you don't let go of your anger and forgive her, you'll never be able to move forward with your own life. Just because this horrible thing has happened to her, it's not your fault. You can't blame yourself for things you can't control."

"As for your father. It sounds like he wasn't equipped to be a parent any more than she was. You have a wonderful family who loves you. Cherish that. If I've learned anything over the years, it's that life is short and precious. You don't want to live with regrets."

I hadn't seen or spoken to him since he'd confirmed my suspicions and turned my life upside down with his final words....

"Yes, Kalli Ballas, I am you father, Michael Conery."

What did those words even mean? He was obviously a different person now, and I was an adult. I had a father already, whom I adored, and worried about how he would feel. But could there be room in my life to get to know my birth father? Did I want to? Did he even want a relationship with me?

Would he leave me again?

So many thoughts kept swirling around in my brain, and I didn't know what to do about any of them. The door opened and Captain Crenshaw, Detective Matheson, and Detective Dreamy all walked in.

"You doing okay?" Nik checked my pupils. He sat down beside me at the long table in the center of the room.

"I'm fine." I folded my hands in front of me, definitely not wanting to be touched at the moment. I could barely handle my own thoughts and wasn't able to deal with anyone else's right now. "Any more news on Elouise?"

I was glad my attacker was off the streets, but I was still in shock that the person who had tried to kill me was Elouise Sinclaire. I never would have suspected that. Secretly, I was proud of myself. I had felt vulnerable ever since the first attack, but after defending myself during the second one, it restored my confidence.

"She didn't come from money like Fay Baker," Boomer said. "She was a self-made, powerful woman from drug money. Ruby not paying up and going on the run threatened Elouise's livelihood. She started unraveling and became obsessed with shutting Ruby up, but she says someone else got to Ruby before she did."

"I could feel so much rage from her every time she looked at me." I shivered, remembering the feeling.

"It's because you look so much like your birth mother," Nik said. "She never did get her money back or her revenge on Ruby. You were the next closest thing for her achieving that. How did you know she was your attacker, by the way?" He eyed me with curiosity and little bit of suspicion if I wasn't mistaken.

"Intuition?" I lied. I would tell him about my gift

when the time was right. Now in front of the others was definitely not the time. "Do you think she's lying? If she murdered Sal and tried to murder me, then she's more than capable of it."

"She sure is," Boomer said. "She was at the Harvest Festival when your Ma broke the latch to the wagon, so she knew it was faulty. And she easily could have followed Ruby back to the park and killed her, setting your Ma up to take the fall. If only she would tell us where she hid the body."

"We're still investigating *all* possible leads," Captain Crenshaw said, reminding me that Ma hadn't been cleared yet, either.

"What about Danny Ferrari?" I asked. "Any more information on him? The other night at the motel he said I knew him."

Nik's gaze locked on mine, and he arched a brow but didn't say anything.

I hadn't had a chance to tell him about that yet, but I would worry about that later. Right now, I needed answers and would do whatever it took to get them. "I don't recognize his name or his look, so I can't imagine how I would know him. We got interrupted when Grayson ran outside and you guys showed up, then Danny was gone."

"Danny Ferrari is his real name," Nik said. "He injured his hand cooking. He's a chef in New York City. His mother's name is Aria Bianchi."

My jaw fell open. "I *do* know him. He own's Aria's Restaurant and goes by Chef Bianchi."

"Correct. It's his way of honoring his late mother," Nik added. "I remember you telling me when you first met with the people from Interludes about your clothing line, they took you to Aria's for dinner."

"Yes, but Danny had on a white chef's uniform and a big hat. I was more concerned with hiding my hand sanitizer and wondering if his silverware was clean, that I barely acknowledged him."

"Well, he obviously had been worried about you recognizing him. That's why he kept looking at you so intensely. He's been in town under his real name, checking out the competition," Nik said. "He met with Thalia and bought a building he plans to use to open a second restaurant."

"That's why I kept seeing him at all the restaurants in town and snooping in Ma's office. He was scoping out the competition. Then I saw him pick up more chef's uniforms from the cleaners and things he might need for the new restaurant from the hardware store, plus he kept receiving packages. It all makes sense now." I puckered my brow. "Why all the secrecy? Why not just tell me who he really was?"

"Are you kidding?" Boomer barked out a laugh. "If your Ma, Vinny, and Rosalita found out Danny was a chef and their future competition, they never would have allowed him to step foot in their restaurants."

"You have a point." I sighed. "That rules him out as a suspect. He obviously didn't even know Ruby Winehouse."

My cell phone rang, and I checked the caller ID.

"Ugh. It's Ma. I have to take this. I'm sure she's heard about my fight with my attacker, finding out about my birth father, and my hospital trip after fainting in the parking lot of Vincenzo's Restaurant." I groaned, dreading the conversation ahead. "This is going to take a lot of explaining to get out of this one."

I answered.

"I'm okay, Ma."

"Well, I'm not." Ma spoke so loudly, everyone in the room could hear her through the phone.

My eyes met Nik's. "I know I have a lot of explaining to do? Doc says I'm okay. My attacker is in jail. And Father's my father."

"Kalli, you no make sense. And you no listen. I need to explain to you. Oh, woe is me. It's the deja dodo all over again."

"Ma, what are you talking about?"

"It's no my fault this time, either. I found the wicked witch, and she's giving me The Evil Eye again. I never gonna be free of this curse."

My heart started pounding and all eyes locked on me as I asked, "Ma, where is Ruby Winehouse?"

"In my freezer."

I STOOD in the back storage room of Aphrodite's Restaurant, staring in shock. Could this day get any crazier? There was an old stand-alone freezer my parents used to use for extra meat, but they hadn't used that in years. They had a state-of-the-art walk-in freezer that had more than enough room for their supplies. They'd talked about getting rid of the old freezer for some time now, but Pop loved to hold onto old things just in case.

Walking up to the open freezer, I was about to peek in when Ma pulled me back. I looked up at her in surprise. "What now?"

"Put these on." She slipped a pair of sunglasses over my eyes. "You no want to get The Evil Eye. Trust me."

I cringed. "Are these glasses sanitized?"

"Go on with you now." She swatted my behind. "Your mama know how to take care of you."

"Okay, jeepers." I stepped forward to join Nik.

He arched a brow at my sunglasses but didn't say a word. "Are you sure you want to do this?"

I nodded. He held my hand and walked up to the freezer with me. For once, he kept his thoughts to himself, thank the Lord. The freezer was plugged in and put on the coldest setting. It definitely hadn't been in the past, so whoever put Ruby's body in here, wanted to keep it preserved.

Mable had closed Ruby's eyes, thank goodness.

I kept my sunglasses on so no one could see my reaction. A huge sense of relief filled me to know I could still do right by Ruby, even if she hadn't done right by me. It was like Father Conery—I couldn't think of him as anything else right now—said, I needed to forgive Ruby to move on with my life.

The CSI team had done their jobs and the body was getting ready to be sent to the coroner's office before being released once more. Wally had stopped by to see for himself that the body had been found. He'd cried in relief and left with Mable.

"You ready?" Nik asked.

"Yes," I responded. "Detective?"

"Hmmm?"

"Thanks for being there for me." I looked up at him and filled my voice with as much feeling as I could. "It means more than you know."

"Always, Ballas." He tweaked my nose then led the way to the front of my parents' restaurant.

"I told you to throw that nasty thing away," Ma said to Pop. "You always hold on to old things. What for? They're worthless."

"You old, but I hold onto you," Pop said.

Ma gaped at him, and I swear, her beehive started buzzing.

"What I say, Ophelia?" He held his hands up and took a step toward her. "Why you look at me that way, my little bumblebee?"

"Don't you bumblebee me, and you no touch me. Maybe not for a long, *long* time." She took a step back and pointed her finger in his face. "Amos Ballas, do you want to make it to forty years of marriage?"

"Yes, that's why I hold onto you." Pop scratched his head. "You no make sense. You so confusing some-times, you make my head hurt. YiaYia, get me some duct tape."

YiaYia stood by Ma's side and crossed her arms.

"Papou?" Pop pleaded, looking like a lost puppy dog.

Papou winced. "Sorry, son, I want to make it to sixty-five years of marriage." He stood by YiaYia.

Frona came out of the washroom, carrying duct tape.

"Ah, finally, someone is on my side." He held out his hand, but Frona ignored it, and proceeded to run circles around him, duct taping his hand to his head in the process.

"Feel better?" Ma asked.

Pop sighed and just stood there with his hand taped to his head. "Whatever you want me to feel, I feel."

"You look like a fool," Ma said but with less anger.

Pop would be forgiven before the dinner rush was over.

"At the risk of ending up in the doghouse like Mr. Ballas, things aren't looking much better for you, Mrs. Ballas," Boomer said.

"Be very careful with your words, Detective." Ma

crossed her arms over her bosom. "I know your mama."

"I'm just saying you're still a suspect in Ruby's death, and now her body is in your freezer. Ruby's not the only thing frozen," Boomer said as gently as he could. "Let's just say your future's been put on ice."

CHAPTER 21

J az and I took Ma to Aunt Tasoula's salon. Her nail tech and aesthetician were all set up and running. She'd even had Jasper install a massage table since the only massage parlor in town had been shut down. My aunt was a smart woman. She knew how to make money.

We walked inside, and the place was standing room only. Her chairs were full with people getting haircuts, the spa was full in back with all three new employees fully booked. The waiting room seats were all taken. Even the pole and—good Lord yes—the swing she'd installed in the other corner were occupied.

"This no relaxing," Ma said. "This a zoo."

Aunt Tasoula motioned us over to a private room off the back.

"You like? I had Jasper leave a little section of my new spa just for me and a few special guests." There were a few plush velvet chairs, a daybed, and a throne rivaling Cleopatra's. There were end tables with magazines, a TV, and a counter with all sorts of snacks and beverages. "I call it my VIP room."

Ma, Chloe, Aunt Tasoula, Jaz and I entered the room. Aunt Tasoula gave up her throne for Ma. She took the daybed. While Chloe, Jaz and I sat in the plush velvet chairs. Aunt Tasoula played hostess and gave us all drinks and plates of assorted foods. My whole family might run various businesses, but they could all cook up a storm.

"Thank you, 'Soula." Ma bit into some Greek hor'-dourves and leaned back on her throne. "This is just what I need." She sipped some strong, black coffee.

"Oh, I got you, 'Phelia." Aunt Tasoula patted Ma's knee. "The curse is strong within you." She spit and tossed a shot of salt.

I ducked. Of course, I had to choose the seat beside the daybed.

"Quincy say no more leads." Chloe shook her head gravely, then tossed back a shot of Ouzo and dabbed the corners of her mouth with a cocktail napkin.

"I'm not giving up hope," I said, sipping my cucumber water and nibbling on a toast point sandwich.

"Boomer said there's still hope that Elouise stole the body and hid it there." Jaz drank a soda and ate some candy.

"I don't know how she would get the body into my freezer without me knowing about it," Ma puckered her brow.

"The woman had her connections." Jaz grunted. "She may not like men, but she loved to use them and was pretty good at it from what I saw."

"I agree," I said. "Until they didn't fall under her charm and give her what she wanted, then she screamed at them like she did Danny Ferrari."

"Don't mention that name. I can't believe he's a chef. He's sneaky. I caught him on my security tape, looking at my new menu additions in my office." Ma scoffed. "Vinny said so, too, when I talked to him."

We all looked at her in surprise.

"So, you're on speaking terms with Vinny now?" I asked.

Ma shrugged. "What? Keep the friends close and the enemies closer. He's the lesser of two evils and an ally right now."

"Does that mean I can eat there now?" Aunt Tasoula asked.

"Don't push your luck, 'Soula."

"I can't keep bringing Tate to your restaurant. It's awkward with you there." My aunt waved her hand about. "And Mexican food gives him the indiscretion. His tummy no take no more."

"Fine, fine," Ma said. "But no one eats at this Danny Ferrari's place, okay? Okay. It's settled." She finished her coffee.

"Want to play a game like we used to as kids?" Aunt Tasoula asked. "I have Life. Or Monopoly."

"I'm living life. It's no great at the moment," Ma grumbled, "and unless you have a Get Out of Jail Free card, then no Monopoly."

A screeching noise sounded throughout the salon, followed by screams and all sorts of crashing noises out in the front of the salon. We all looked at each other and ran out of the room. YiaYia Dido was tangled up in the swing. Frona had pulled the fire alarm. The sprinklers had turned on, and all the customers went running.

"I told you not to buy that swing," Ma said, pointing her finger at Aunt Tasoula. "You no listen."

"My salon," Aunt Tasoula wailed. "I no sure even Jasper can fix this."

We untangled YiaYia, wrangled Frona, and then

ran outside with everyone else. My cell phone rang, and I checked the caller ID. "It's Nik," I said to the group and then answered.

I listened to him talk, my eyes growing bigger with every word, then I told him I would be right there and hung up.

"What was that about?" Jaz asked.

I looked at Aunt Tasoula. "You'll have to find someone else to fix this mess. Jasper Kent has just been arrested for Ruby's murder and the stealing and hiding of her body." Then I looked at Ma. "Guess you just found your Get Out of Jail Free card."

~

"WHERE DO I GO?" I walked into the police station and joined Nik.

"Follow me to my office first, and I'll fill you in." He led the way to his office, and I followed.

I sat down. "What exactly happened?"

"The CSI guys found Jasper's DNA on Ruby's body. He didn't even try to deny taking her and hiding her in the freezer, but he swears he didn't kill her. We're keeping him in a holding cell while he waits for his attorney."

"Why am I here?"

"He says he won't talk to anyone but you and only you."

"I don't understand why, but okay."

"Maybe it's because you're Ruby's next of kin? I'm not really sure." Nik looked at me with concern. "You don't have to do this, you know."

"I know. I want to. I'm actually curious what he has to say." I took a deep breath. "Lead the way, Detective."

"You got it, Ballas. We moved him to an 8 x 10 interrogation room to talk to you. It's near the suspect processing area. Moving a suspect through the station poses an unnecessary risk, and I won't take any risks with you."

I followed him out of his office, and we came to a room. He hesitated with his hand on the doorknob. "Remember, I'll be right outside this door if you need me."

I nodded, and he opened the door.

I walked inside the small room. There was a table in the center with chairs around it, recording equipment, and a white board. Nothing was being recorded, it was just Jasper and me. I sat in a chair across from him, not sure what to say.

"Hey, Kalli. How are you?" He asked quietly, still wearing his normal day clothes of jeans, a sweatshirt, and work boots.

"I'm fine. The bigger question is, how are you?" I watched him carefully.

"I'm not gonna lie. I've been better."

"I don't understand what happened, Jasper. I'm normally a good judge of character. Everyone likes you, and you've helped so many people around town. You just don't seem like the kind of person who could commit murder."

He looked me in the eye and said with such sincerity, "I'm not a murderer, Kalli. I can promise you that."

"Then what are you?"

He paused for so long I didn't think he was going to speak. He swallowed hard, his Adam's apple bobbing, then he finally said, "I'm your brother."

Shock coursed through me, and I sat frozen to my chair, unable to utter a single word for several moments.

"Are you okay? Should I call Detective Stevens in?" Jasper asked.

He looked at me with genuine concern. I stared into his eyes. Green eyes. Eyes just like Ruby and my own, and the truth sank in.

"You're my brother," I breathed.

He seemed to wilt with relief that I believed him. "Half-brother, actually. Ruby is our mother, but we have different father's."

"Okay, I'm gonna need a minute." I went to the door and opened it.

"What's wrong?" Nik asked.

"I need water. Bring two glasses, please."

"You sure you're okay?"

"I'm fine. I'll fill you in later, but water please. Quickly. Thank you." I closed the door in his face, still in shock, and returned my seat. "Okay, start from the beginning."

"Ruby had you when she was really young. I had no idea who your biological father was until just the other day. One time with Father Conery was all it took to create you, I guess."

"Apparently, so."

The door opened, and Nik came in with a pitcher of water and two glasses. He set it down in the center of the table, stood up and looked at us both a couple times. We just sat there, waiting patiently until he frowned and walked away. Jasper didn't speak until Nik closed the door behind him.

"The way I heard it, your father freaked out after being with Ruby because of his issues and left because he couldn't handle a relationship. He didn't even find out she was pregnant until she'd already given you up, and by then it was too late. Sorry about that. He seems like a nice guy now, but I think back then he was a whole different person."

"So, I've heard. I'm grateful they gave me up. I've had an amazing life so far with Ophelia and Amos Ballas."

"I know you have. You're lucky. I wasn't."

"What happened?"

"I came along two years after you. Ruby fell in love and thought the guy loved her back. She got pregnant and really thought he'd marry her. He was her ticket out of the hellhole she'd been living." Jasper shrugged. "He loved *her* but not me. He couldn't handle being a father, so he split."

"What did Ruby do?"

"She kept me for five years, hoping he would change his mind. He didn't. I never met him, and he never came back. So, she threw me out like trash. I was never adopted, living in an orphanage and foster homes that were cruel. I've been on my own since I was eighteen. I changed my name from Jasper Winehouse to Jasper Kent. I'd always wanted superman to be my father, hoping I would become a better man than my real father."

"Oh, Jasper, I'm so sorry." I touched his hand and felt his sincerity. *I hated her so much, but I didn't kill her. Why won't anyone believe me?* "I believe you."

He blinked and pulled his hand away, looking confused. "Did I just speak my thoughts out loud?"

"I could tell what you were thinking. It's written all over your face," I said, not ready to reveal that part of myself to him just yet.

"Anyway, I found a way to survive on my own. I'd pretty much been doing it my whole life. I became good at a lot of odd jobs and found I could make money that way. For a while I moved around a lot, but then I saw your face on the news. I knew right away who you were. You look just like her."

"I know. It's kind of creepy."

"For me, too. It was hard for me to look at you at first, but you're so much different than she was. You're nice and you actually care about people. Anyway, when I got here, I did some work at the Clearview Motel and ran into Ruby. She didn't even recognize me. That hurt more than anything."

"I can only imagine."

"I wanted to confront her and tell her how I felt about everything she had done to me, but it was never a good time. Then suddenly someone murdered her. I was so angry. I felt robbed. I never got the chance to say my peace."

"She wouldn't have cared. I tried to talk to her, but all she wanted from me was money. She didn't want to know me at all."

"It might not have mattered to her, but it mattered to me. And then when they declared you her next of kin, I knew I would look crazy coming forward with a different last name and no connection to her for so long. Besides, you're older than me so it would have been your choice what to do with her body anyway."

"I believe you didn't murder her, and I'm sorry you didn't get the chance to say your peace, but why steal her body? How did that even come about?"

"When I was doing work for Mr. Newcomer at the funeral home. I saw an opportunity when they were all gone, and I didn't think about it. I acted out of frustration and anger."

"What did you plan to do with her?"

"I wanted to throw her out in the landfill like trash. Show her how much she was worth, just like she showed us." He sighed. "That was anger talking. I couldn't go through with it. But at that point, I had no clue how I was going to sneak a body back into the morgue. Wally pretty much put everyone on lockdown, not willing to take a chance of anything like that happening again. I had to put Ruby somewhere that she wouldn't decompose before I made things right and returned her to you to decide what to do with her."

"When Ma asked you to do some odd jobs for her and you saw the old freezer, the perfect solution presented itself I take it."

He nodded. "I promise I took good care of Ruby. I handled her carefully and put her in the best position I possibly could in that freezer. I was going to come clean. I just didn't know how or when or what to say."

"That was quite a shock for Ma to find her body."

"I was actually relieved when Ruby's body was found, and this nightmare was over. I feel bad your mother was the one to find her. Your parents are great people. They've treated me like a member of the family. I've never had that."

"This isn't over, Jasper." I squeezed his hand. "I'm going to find a good lawyer, not the court appointed one they will stick you with. We're going to fight this. I'm sure you'll have to do some time, but I think given all you've been through at Ruby's hands, a judge will go lenient on you."

He stared at me long and hard, his eyes, so similar to mine, filling with tears. "Y-You would do that for me?"

"I would do that for family." I smiled through my own tears. "We're family, Jasper. Don't you forget that."

"What are you going to do?"

"Find out who really killed our mother."

CHAPTER 22

News got out that Jasper was my half-brother, and the next morning, all the Greeks from both Nik and my families came together and raised money for a lawyer. Thalia knew a lot of powerful people back in New York City. She used her connections and got a high-powered attorney to drop everything and take this case.

Only the gods knew what she promised him.

Now that I knew my brother was going to be okay, I pulled into the parking lot of Newcomer Funeral Home to take care of some long overdue business and turned off my Prius. It was early morning. The sun was shining, the air was crisp, and colorful leaves were falling. It was going to be a beautiful day.

Finally, something was going right.

"Hi, Wally, thanks for agreeing to open up early for me," I said as I walked through the front door.

"No problem at all." He smiled and led the way into his office. "I'm glad to make up for losing Ruby's body in the first place." He frowned as he sat behind his desk. "I'm shocked that Jasper was the one who took her, but it did cause me to up my security to prevent something like that from every happening again."

The room was comfortable. A calming blue with plush cream chairs, a few plants, and a water cooler in the corner. I liked that the water was free of chemicals and the paper cups sanitized in the metal sleeve, so it was never touched except by the person pulling one out. I poured a cup and sat down across from Wally.

"I'm not saying what Jasper did was right, but he's been through a lot in his life," I finally responded with a shrug. "That kind of trauma can make a person do things that are out of character."

"I've heard his story, and I can understand why." Wally nodded. "Ruby certainly stirred up a lot of drama in the short time she was here."

"That's an understatement, but she *is* my birth mother. Jasper's, too. I believe he didn't kill her. There's still the possibility that Elouise did. That woman is pure evil." I shivered, in shock that she could take someone's life so easily.

"There are still rumors that Ophelia killed Ruby, but I know that's not the case. Your mother is a good person. She's always been so kind to me." He smiled fondly. "Since the moment we met in kindergarten, she has been my friend. I just hate to see her go through any of this. She doesn't deserve it."

"Ma's a strong woman. She won't go down without a fight, and neither will I." I sat up straight and took a sip of water before adding proudly, "I got that from her."

His whole face softened. "Your mother is a special woman, indeed."

Affection laced his tone and had me looking at him more closely and seeing him in a whole new light. If I wasn't mistaken, I would swear he had feelings for

Ma. Had he always? For all these years? The poor man didn't stand a chance against Pop, not to mention, he wasn't Greek. He probably knew that, but to pine away for someone for so long and have your love unrequited was so sad.

He pushed his glasses up further on his nose. "Have you decided what you want to do with Ruby's remains?" he asked, snapping me out of my thoughts. My eyes met his, and he gave me a funny look before adding, "We're running out of time."

I couldn't worry about Wally's feelings for Ma. I had a body to bury and a murder to solve. I took a deep breath and focused. "Jasper and I talked, and we would like to have her cremated."

Wally wrote down a few notes in his booking ledger. "When would you like to schedule this?"

"As soon as possible."

"What about a ceremony?" He looked back up at me. "And do you want her ashes buried?"

"No ceremony and no ashes buried. When Jasper gets out of jail, we want to have my biological father, Father Conery, say something since he knew her the best. Then we'll spread her ashes somewhere special to her so she can finally be at peace." I accidentally knocked my water over, and we both reached for the cup at the same time, our hands touching.

That horrible woman doesn't deserve to be at peace after what she put my Ophelia through.

I yanked my hand back and gaped at him.

He frowned. "What's wrong?"

"You killed Ruby."

His face paled. "H-How did you know?" He stood. "I-It was an accident."

I bolted to my feet, keeping the table between us. "Don't come near me."

He held up his hands, looking sad. "I'm not going to hurt you."

"I don't believe you."

He sighed and sat back down. "I never meant for any of this to happen."

I slowly sat back down as well. "Then why did you do it?"

His eyes met mine, and I could see the sincerity and regret.

"You love Ma, don't you?"

He nodded. "Ever since we were kids. She was the only person who was kind to me. I knew she didn't love me back, but we were friends. I was content with that."

"What happened?"

"Ruby Winehouse came to town." Anger and a little disgust transformed his face. "You are the center or your mother's universe. I live to see her happy. So, for this monster to come to town and remind Ophelia that you have a birth mother is just wrong. The adoption was supposed to be closed."

I just sat there and waited for him to continue.

The anger seeped out of him, and he looked tired. And stressed. Ma was right. He had grown thinner. "Anyway, when I found out Ruby was demanding money from you and your mother to go away for good, I knew she never would. Bribe money never works."

"I told Ma that, but she didn't listen."

"I didn't know your mother had agreed to meet Ruby at the park. I followed Ruby and was surprised when she went to the park so late at night."

"What happened next?"

"I found Ruby waiting by the wagon. I wasn't at the park earlier, so I didn't see your mother play with the latch. I didn't know it was faulty. I pleaded with Ruby to do the right thing and leave town. I usually have a way with people, but she wouldn't listen to reason." His eyes met mine. "I didn't mean to break the latch. I was nervous and started fiddling with it when all of a sudden, it came loose. Tons of harvested fruits and vegetables came tumbling out right on top of her. Just her feet were sticking out, but they weren't moving."

"Why didn't you call the police right away?" I studied him.

He held up his hands. "I panicked, so I did what I always do?"

"What's that?"

"He called me," said a voice from behind me.

I whirled around in my seat and saw Mable Griffith standing in the doorway and holding a gun pointed right at my head.

~

"WHERE ARE YOU TAKING US?" I asked.

Mable had forced both Wally and me into the back of his hearse then stole the keys and was driving us to Zeus only knew where.

"What are you doing, Mable?" Wally asked through the open glass to the front seats. "This isn't going to end well for any of us."

"I'm keeping you from confessing to the world now just like I did when you called me the first time." Her voice didn't sound anything like the shy, quiet Mable I was used to.

"What we did was wrong. Ruby might have still been alive if we had called the police right away."

"You don't know that for sure. And she would have still been blackmailing your precious Ophelia for money. I saved you from that."

"And by doing so, you set Ophelia up to take the fall for what started out as a simple accident. If I hadn't called you, I *would* have called the police."

Mable was already shaking her head. "You would have gone to jail, Wally. I couldn't let that happen."

"Why?"

"Because she loves you like you love Ma," I said, everything suddenly clear to me.

Mable was going through the same unrequited love with Wally that Wally was going through with Ma. It made me realize if I got out of this alive, I was going to make sure Nik knew I loved him, too, and I would give anything to be official right now.

Wally's eyes widened as my words sank in. "Is this true, Mable?"

"Of course, it's true, but you're so blinded by your obsession with a woman who will never love you back, that you ignored a woman who worshipped you that was right in front of your face. I thought that, if Ophelia took the fall and was out of the picture, you would finally be free from the spell she has over you." She shook her head and sadness filled her voice. "We could have had it all, but you would rather be alone and miserable."

"I don't know what to say," he replied quietly, looking a little lost.

"Say you'll run away with me, and I'll forgive you." Her voice refilled with hope.

"I can't, Mable." His eyes met mine. "I'm through running. I'm going to the police."

She looked in the rear-view-mirror, and her eyes hardened as she glared at me. Just like Elouise hated me for being Ruby's biological daughter, Mable hated me for being Ophelia's only child and more important to Wally than her.

"No, you're not," she said with a deadly tone. "I'm not going to take the fall with you. If I can't have you, then no one can."

Wally looked at her with alarm. "What are you going to do?"

"Bury you with your love's child," Mable spat, her face transforming into someone I didn't even recognize. "Maybe you'll finally rest in peace then."

"Mable, you can't be serious."

"Oh, I'm deadly serious. I'm a coroner. I know exactly where to shoot you so you will die quickly and won't feel a thing." Her gaze shot to me. "Her, on the other hand, I might let die slowly. Someone has to suffer like I have for so long."

Wally kept talking to Mable and trying to convince her to turn back. She was headed out of town on a back road with no other cars around. While he talked, I looked around the back of the hearse. I had to do something.

I spotted a small toolkit in the corner. Carefully opening it, I found a long screwdriver. I located the release latch and stuck the screwdriver inside, then pressed on the trigger to release the latch. The doors flew open just like how my Pop had shown me when I first got my license, in case I ever got locked out or in a car.

"Hey, what are you doing?" Mable yelled and hit the brakes, sending Wally flying into the glass separating the back from the front.

I jumped out the back at the same time that she hit the brakes and rolled as I hit the ground like I'd been taught by Ma, yelping along the way. I was going to be sore tomorrow for sure.

The hearse stopped up ahead and Wally scrambled out of the back. Mable opened the front door, but

Wally jumped on her as she raised her gun. The gun went off, and Wally grunted, then fell to the ground in a heap.

Mable stood there shaking and sobbing. She dropped the gun and fell to the ground beside him. "Wally? Oh, please be alive. Wally, talk to me. I didn't mean what I said." She felt for a pulse and cried harder when she found one. "Call the police, Kalli."

"I don't have my phone."

"Mine's in the front seat. Call the police, now!"

"But I thought you were going to kill us. I thought you didn't care if he died?"

"I lied. Now call the police before I change my mind."

I ran back to the hearse, kicked her gun out of the way, and then grabbed her phone off the front seat and called Nik. He answered on the first ring.

"Where are you? I saw your car at the funeral home, but no one was there, and the hearse was missing. We've all been combing the town, looking for you and Wally."

"Mable Griffith kidnapped us, and Wally's been shot."

"What? I'll send an ambulance. Give me the address."

"We're on route eleven about five miles past the town line."

He called it in over his police radio, and then said to me, "That was the next place I was going to look. I'll be there in five minutes."

"Wait, Detective, don't hang up yet."

"Why? Are you okay?"

"No."

"What's wrong?"

"I love you."

I heard his engine rev. "I'll be there in two." Then the line went dead.

True to his word, he made it in two minutes, and the ambulance and other police cars arrived a few minutes later. I filled them all in on what happened. Wally was taken to the hospital while Mable was arrested and taken to jail for a whole slew of crimes. She was sobbing incoherently and babbling about nonsense. She would be evaluated by mental health officials as well. Wally was awake and confessed his crime. He would undoubtedly face some time, but at least he was alive. Love made people crazy. I was a mess.

I had confessed mine, and Nik hadn't said a word.

Nik drove me home and called for someone to tow my car home. He pulled in the driveway and cut the engine and just sat there.

"Say something, please."

He looked at me with tears in his eyes and raw emotion shining bright. "You love me. I wasn't even sure you still *liked* me. And here you love me?"

"Is that okay?" I asked as tears filled my eyes, too.

He laughed softly. "That's more than okay. I love you, too, Ballas. So damn much." He kissed me, and I felt the truth of his words. *Please tell me we're official now. And can we please move in together so I can wake up next to your beautiful face every day?*

I pulled away long enough to say, "Yes and no. Baby steps, Detective, and for the record, I think your face is beautiful, too."

"How did you...?"

"I read your mind." I shrugged, then kissed him again.

EPILOGUE

"Hello, girlfriend," Nik said as we sat curled up on my couch together. *You have a spider on your—*

"Hey!" I started to jump up.

"Just making sure you're paying attention." He winked.

"Not funny, boyfriend. I never should have told you I could read minds."

"I think it's amazing." He kissed the top of my head. *I think you're amazing.*

"You're not so bad yourself."

He chuckled. "I still can't believe a bump on the head gave you that ability, and it's a bit unfair. Now, I have to watch what I'm thinking when I'm touching you, but you can think whatever you want."

"Then don't touch me."

"Not a chance. I'd rather bite my tongue...or thoughts."

We'd gotten in the habit of rotating houses, pretty much waking up together on a daily basis anyway, but I drew the line at knocking down the wall that separated our half of the houses. Sharing one house with both our pets and learning to live with each other's habits I wasn't quite ready for yet.

But I had to admit being official pretty much rocked.

"I'm so glad Winnie is home with Kosmos, finally. They say she should make a full recovery," I said.

"I'm so glad your Ma's name is cleared, and her Evil Eye curse is gone. It makes my job much more boring, which I'll gladly take."

"Guess What! When Jasper gets out, he agreed to stay in Clearview. Ma and Pop want to adopt him, even though he's twenty-seven. He said yes. I'm so happy."

"That's great, Kalli. I'm really happy for you." Sincerity rang out in his voice, warming my insides. "I heard Father Conery is taking over for Father Comstock permanently. How do you feel about that?"

"I'm okay with it. Pop knows I love him, and he'll always be my father. It will be nice to get to know Father Conery better, but I promised Ma I would not change churches."

"Wally will make a full recovery as well. He'll do time, but I think everyone knows he acted with good intentions. They'll forgive him and he'll be back when he gets out. As for Mable, she's getting the help she needs." *Now, what's for dinner?*

"Just for that, you're cooking."

"Great. I know exactly what I want." He stood up and scooped me into his arms and headed down the hall. *Breakfast in bed.*

"My favorite," I said.

I guess reading minds wasn't so bad after all.

ABOUT THE AUTHOR

Kari Lee Townsend is a National Bestselling Author of mysteries & a tween superhero series. She also writes romance and women's fiction as Kari Lee Harmon. With a background in English education, she's now a full-time writer, wife to her own superhero, mom of 3 sons, 1 darling diva, 1 daughter-in-law & 2 lovable fur babies. These days you'll find her walking her dogs or hard at work on her next story, living a blessed life.

BOOKS BY KARI LEE
TOWNSEND

BOOKS BY KARI LEE HARMON

FROZEN WATERS (COLDWATER COVE #2)

Dark Seas (Coldwater Cove #1)

Valley of Secrets

Until Tomorrow

Jingle all the Way (Merry Scroog-mas novella #3)

Sleigh Bells Ring (Merry Scroog-mas novella #2)

Naughty or Nice (Merry Scroog-mas novella #1)

Brook (Lakehouse Treasures novella #4)

Meghan (Lakehouse Treasure novella #3)

Amber (Lakehouse Treasures novella #2)

James (Lakehouse Treasures novella #1)

Sleeping in the Middle (Comfort Club #1)

Love Lessons

Project Produce

Spurred by Fate (Triple R Ranch short story #2)

Destiny Wears Spurs (Triple R Ranch #1)

* 9 7 8 1 6 4 8 3 9 3 1 0 5 *